She had come at him like a .... for a steel door. The force from .... pushed him back two steps. It knocked the wind out of him and caused the brooch pinned over her heart to dig into his chest.

After living with people who would not notice, or care, if he went missing, Randy welcomed Cass's enthusiasm. He dropped the coat slung over his arm and embraced his wife. Despite the presence of his in-laws, his lips pressed against hers.

Randy relished the feel of her curves against his body. He had awakened too many mornings without her by his side and had gone to sleep too often with his arms longing to hold her.

Six years earlier, when he stood before the justice of the peace in the presence of their friends and agreed to take Cass as his wife, he had done so with the intention of letting no man separate them physically, as well as in his heart. But when he received his draft notice, he had been given little choice. He either had to serve his country or go into hiding, facing jail time.

The two years he had been away had been the longest and loneliest of his life. He wanted to reassure Cass of his devotion to her and make up for the nights they had been unable to come together.

The sound of a throat clearing pierced through the mental shield Randy had erected to block out everyone but his wife. The reminder that they were not alone did not diminish Randy's desire for Cass. But out of respect for those present, he broke the kiss.

Cass buried her head in his shoulder. The tears he had seen in her eyes before she closed the gap between them soaked his collar.

Praise for Ursula Renée

"*SWEET JAZZ* hits the right notes as historical fiction with romantic elements."
>*~Ann Fitzgerald, InD'Scribe*

~*~

"*SWEET JAZZ*…is a sweet romantic story that like jazz has propulsive rhythms played out in harmonic freedom."
>*~Ginger, Long and Short Reviews*

Bitter Blues

by

Ursula Renée

The Big Band Series, Book 2

This is a work of fiction. Names, characters, places, and incidents are either the product of the author's imagination or are used fictitiously, and any resemblance to actual persons living or dead, business establishments, events, or locales, is entirely coincidental.

Bitter Blues

COPYRIGHT © 2017 by Ursula Renée

All rights reserved. No part of this book may be used or reproduced in any manner whatsoever without written permission of the author or The Wild Rose Press, Inc. except in the case of brief quotations embodied in critical articles or reviews.
Contact Information: info@thewildrosepress.com

Cover Art by *Rae Monet, Inc. Design*

The Wild Rose Press, Inc.
PO Box 708
Adams Basin, NY 14410-0708
Visit us at www.thewildrosepress.com

Publishing History
First Mainstream Historical Rose Edition, 2017
Print ISBN 978-1-5092-1510-2
Digital ISBN 978-1-5092-1511-9

The Big Band Series, Book 2
Published in the United States of America

Dedication

This is dedicated to my little muse,
who continually pushes me to follow my dreams.

Chapter 1

November 1945

Squeezing three women into a kitchen built for one was a recipe for disaster.

Though Cassie Ann Porter had foreseen trouble when her mother insisted Martha Lynn help prepare Thanksgiving dinner, she shushed the little voice inside her head that chanted, "I told you so," as a dozen cookies rained down onto the floor.

The clang of the metal tray smacking the wood floor vibrated off the walls. Martha Lynn flung the towel she had used in place of a potholder on top of the mess. With the same mouth she'd used to kiss Cass's brother on their wedding day, she repeated a four-letter word that began with an F and rhymed with duck, while she stomped her size-seven pump.

A "humph" drowned out the last two letters of the offensive word as it spilled from her lips a fourth time. Martha Lynn's foot froze in midair. Her eyes grew wide, and her mouth formed into an O. She hesitated a heartbeat before she peeked over her shoulder at her mother-in-law.

Sarah Porter rose from the stool where she had been perched to the feet she had been standing on for six hours while preparing the side dishes. Her round eyes squinted, and her full lips turned down until her face was contorted into a menacing grimace. She placed her hands on her hips, and her soft-sole shoe tapped the floor as she glared at the woman who dared to use profanity in her presence.

"I'm sor...I didn't...I mean...I think I hear June calling for me," Martha Lynn stammered.

The sweet melody of her youngest child's laughter drifted from the adjacent house, indicating neither the child nor anyone one else had summoned the woman. Yet despite the lie, Martha Lynn backed away until she collided with the wall. She slid along the surface until her hand touched air. Then, with a high-pitched squeak, she darted out of the kitchen.

The hens in the fenced-in pen behind the house squawked as their peace was disturbed by Martha Lynn's pumps slapping the steps that led from the back porch to the ground.

As the younger woman's footsteps faded around the corner of the house, the matriarch of the Porter family spun around and shook a calloused finger at Cass. "Don't...say...a...word."

Cass mimed zipping her lips and shook her head. Her insistence on speaking her mind had led to more confrontations than her family cared to remember, but even she was not bold enough to point out the flaw in her mother's plan to have Martha Lynn help with the meal. Though the older woman barely reached five feet, she would not hesitate to grab a broom and chase after anyone who vexed her.

"What was I thinkin'?" Her mother picked the tray off the floor and carried it to the other side of the room.

"That Martha Lynn should contribute something to the meal we're preparing for *her* husband," Cass replied as she grabbed the straw broom from the corner opposite the stove.

Under normal circumstances, no one would ask Martha Lynn to help with a meal. The woman was useless when it came to housework and could not point out a stove if it was the only item in the room. However, four hours into the preparations, Cass's mother had suggested the woman bake a dessert for her husband, who had been overseas for two years.

Martha Lynn spent the next two hours not only demonstrating her lack of skills but a lack of interest in what she was doing. Her attitude had been reminiscent of the one she displayed whenever Cass asked her sister-in-law to help out around the apartment the two women shared in the city while doing their part for the war effort. Not once had the woman lent a hand without a complaint or a calamity.

"I should've known better than to expect anythin' from that chile," her mother mumbled under her breath as she dropped the tray into the basin that sat on a shelf. "Never could understand what Joe Frank saw in that lazy, behind girl."

Cass silently snorted. When they were younger, Martha Lynn distracted boys with a toss of her fine hair, a bat of her long lashes over her hazel eyes, and a switch of her full hips. There had been rumors she did not tease those who fell under her spell but delivered the promised goods. Therefore, it neither surprised Cass that her brother sampled what had been offered nor that the evidence of the ride appeared nine months later.

"By the way, you see that letter I left for you next to the radio?" her mother asked.

Cass rolled her eyes as she swept up the cookies to

add them to the slop bucket on the floor under the table.

"I saw that. But I guess I deserved it." Her mother sighed. "That question was crazier than me suggestin' Martha Lynn help out. Bet it was first thin' you saw when you walked in the house last night."

While Cass looked forward to the letters she received from her husband, it had been the second thing she saw when she arrived at her parents' farm. The first thing she sought out each week when she returned from the city were the two beautiful results of her husband's demonstrations of his love.

As difficult as it was for her to be separated from her husband, it was equally as hard to leave her girls each Sunday to drive to Norfolk, Virginia, where she worked during the week. She managed only by reminding herself they could use the additional income, she was doing her part for the war effort, and she would return to her daughters Friday evening.

With her daughters being her first priority, Cass would dole out hugs and kisses before she listened as they gave her an update on their week. She would then read them a story, listen to their prayers, and put them to bed.

Once the girls were tucked in for the night, she would grab the letter from the cabinet that sat next to the back door.

"Anythin' new?" her mother asked.

"He has six more months." Cass tried to keep her voice steady despite the lump that formed in the back of her throat each time she remembered the words scribbled on the paper.

It had taken a considerable amount of self-control after reading the letter not to toss it across the room and throw herself on the floor and kick and scream at the unfairness of it all. Uncle Sam had already had her husband for over twenty-four months. It was past time he stopped being selfish and sent her man home.

"I'm sorry, baby." Her mother patted her arm. "I know it's hard."

Cass glanced at the woman whose dark brown hair showed no traces of gray despite her fifty-nine years. Though her mother meant well, Cass did not believe the woman knew what she was going through.

During their forty-plus years of marriage, her parents had never been separated for more than the eight hours her father spent working at the mill. That was a big difference from being away from a husband for two years.

Though she wanted to be a good American, she wanted her husband home. Hell, she'd never wanted him to leave in the first place. When he received the letter telling him to report for duty, she had thought someone was playing a joke on them. Yet a trip to the recruitment office confirmed that the government wanted him, despite being a husband and father in his thirties.

Cass squeezed the hand on her arm before she continued to sweep up the mess. The crunch of gravel under tires drifted through the doors they'd left open to get relief from the hot stove.

"That's gotta be Joe Frank." Her mother clapped her hands together and turned her eyes upward. "Thank you for seein' my boy home safe." She glanced toward Cass. Tears of joy filled her eyes. "Come say hi to your brother."

"I'll be there in a minute."

Her mother nodded before rushing out of the extension her father had added behind the house twenty years earlier so his wife would have more space to move about as she prepared meals for the family of eight. The structure had seemed enormous to Cass's nine-year-old perspective, but after living in apartments that were twice the size of her childhood home, she found the space smaller than she was used to.

Despite the cramped quarters, she enjoyed preparing meals with her mother in the kitchen where the aroma of freshly baked bread and hearty meals hung in the air. She hoped one day her children would have fond memories of working next to her.

"Mercy." Her mother's voice rose over the chatter in the house. "Cassie Ann, get in here."

Cass had hoped she'd be given another minute before she was forced to plaster on a smile and be sociable. As much as she loved Joe Frank, who was closer in age to her than their other brothers, she would have preferred to be greeting her husband.

She pulled off her apron and draped it over the back of a chair, then checked her reflection in the blade of a butter knife. Her eyes glistened with unshed tears, but she figured she could call them happy tears, and with any luck, everyone would be too busy celebrating her brother's return to recognize the lie.

"Hurry up."

She tossed the knife onto the table. "I'm comin'." Her accent became thicker, betraying her emotions. "Don't know what all the fussin's about. It's only Joe."

A deep chuckle preceded the heavy tread of someone approaching the back door. "Some thin's never change."

Cass froze in the doorway at the voice she had not expected to hear for months. She had once read that longing too much for something could make a person hear things that weren't there. Yet before she could question her sanity, the soldier stepped onto the back porch.

Forgetting the respect she had for her mother and the presence of young ears, Cass uttered an expletive as she rushed forward.

Chapter 2

She had come at him like a battering ram aiming for a steel door. The force from the impact pushed him back two steps. It knocked the wind out of him and caused the brooch pinned over her heart to dig into his chest.

After living with people who would not notice, or care, if he went missing, Randy welcomed Cass's enthusiasm. He dropped the coat slung over his arm and embraced his wife. Despite the presence of his in-laws, his lips pressed against hers.

Randy relished the feel of her curves against his body. He had awakened too many mornings without her by his side and had gone to sleep too often with his arms longing to hold her.

Six years earlier, when he stood before the justice of the peace in the presence of their friends and agreed to take Cass as his wife, he had done so with the intention of letting no man separate them physically, as well as in his heart. But when he received his draft notice, he had been given little choice. He either had to serve his country or go into hiding, facing jail time.

The two years he had been away had been the longest and loneliest of his life. He wanted to reassure Cass of his devotion to her and make up for the nights they had been unable to come together.

The sound of a throat clearing pierced through the

mental shield Randy had erected to block out everyone but his wife. The reminder that they were not alone did not diminish Randy's desire for Cass. But out of respect for those present, he broke the kiss.

Cass buried her head in his shoulder. The tears he had seen in her eyes before she closed the gap between them soaked his collar. His own tears rushed down his cheeks.

"Told you she wouldn't miss you," his brother-in-law called from inside the house. "How 'bout we go to the juke joint and get a drink?"

"You're not going anywhere."

Cass's mumbled reply was unnecessary. After being away for two years, four months, and twenty-seven days, he had no intention of leaving her anytime soon. Hell, she would be lucky if he let her out of his sight long enough for her to visit the outhouse.

"I wouldn't dream of it," Randy reassured her before kissing the top of her head.

The peck was as chaste as the kiss he would give to his mother-in-law. Yet an energy shot straight to his groin, awakening the part of his body that had been denied a woman's warm touch during his time away from Cass.

"You're not going away again?" A voice that was transitioning from its high-pitched, childish squeak to the deeper tone of an adult, drifted from inside the house. Her question diverted his attention from thoughts he could not entertain until Cass and he were alone in the small bedroom they used whenever they visited her parents.

Randy glanced over his shoulder and through the crowd that had gathered to welcome the youngest son of Mack and Sarah Porter home. His brother-in-law stood by the front door, where his daughter had attached herself to his waist. Tears coated his round lenses.

The man's brown hand brushed the girl's wavy, reddish-brown hair that was pulled back into a ponytail. "Not if I can help it," Joe Frank replied.

With a smile that brightened the sunlit room, the girl laid her head on her father's chest. The lines that creased her forehead quickly faded.

A younger girl stood to the side. Her tense posture and the confusion in her eyes said she did not know what to make of the stranger with her sister, and she was waiting for instructions on how to proceed. Instead of easing the girl's fears, Martha Lynn stood in the corner of the room, chewing gum and twirling the ends of her loose hair around a finger.

The children reminded Randy of the girls he had caught a glimpse of as he rushed through the house to get to Cass. His gaze moved around the room that served as the family's living room, dining room, and spare bedroom, until he located the cherubs peeping from behind their grandmother at him.

Both girls were a shade lighter than their mother's medium-brown complexion. Each of them possessed her high cheekbones and full lips, yet they had inherited Randy's green eyes.

They each wore their thick, curly, dark brown hair in two braids with ribbons securing the ends. The older girl, two inches taller than her sister, wore a pink dress, while the younger wore yellow. And, like their mother, they wore ankle socks and canvas shoes.

Randy pulled away from Cass and dropped to his

knees in front of the back door. The last time he had been home, one girl had just turned three and the other had yet to be born.

"Sylvia...Shara...come say hi to your daddy." Cass waved the girls over.

Sylvia, who had been named after the wife of Randy's mentor, inched farther behind her grandmother, her eyes wide with fear. Her younger sister shook her head; her lips were pursed tight, and she had a defiant glare in her eyes.

Randy spread his arms out. "Don't be afraid." Though he softened his tone, it still sounded loud, thanks to the hush that fell over the room.

"No." Shara buried her face in the ankle-length skirt of the woman she had been named after.

"Sylvia...Shara...didn't you hear me tell you come here?" Cass stepped around Randy and into the house.

The older girl's lip quivered, and her sister mewled. The sound tore through Randy's heart. As much as he wanted to hold both his daughters in his arms, he did not want to be the cause of their distress.

He grabbed Cass's hand. "It's okay," he said.

"I don't know what's gotten into them," she replied.

"They're not used to him," Mother Porter said, swinging Shara onto her hip. The girl laid her head on the woman's shoulder and shoved her thumb in her mouth. "Give 'em time."

"But—" Cass started to protest.

Randy dropped his arms to his side and stood. "She's right." Despite the sting from their rejection, he forced the corners of his lips to remain up.

Cass's brow wrinkled. "I don't know what

happened. I showed them your picture and told them about you."

He had no doubt she'd done what she could to assure the girls knew who he was. But unlike Joe Frank's eldest daughter, both of his girls were too young to remember him.

"Your mother's right. It'll take time." He reached out and brushed her cheek. "They'll have years to get used to me. Not like I'm goin' anywhere…ever."

"You better not." Cass squeezed his hand.

"Cassie Ann said you weren't comin' home for another six months," Mother Porter announced.

"They mixed up my papers with someone else's." He draped an arm around Cass's shoulders. "When I found out, I decided to surprise you."

"Surprised me when he stepped off that train in D.C.," Joe Frank said as he shrugged out of his coat, a task not made easy by the girl who refused to release him.

"Glad I bumped into him. I had someone to talk to on the ride down."

"How was that possible?" Cass asked.

"Conductor didn't question me when I told him Joe was my brother-in-law." By offering no further details, he had been able to ride in the "Colored" car from D.C. to Rocky Mount, where Cass's eldest sibling had been waiting to drive Joe Frank to Piney Woods.

"Boy, sometimes you act like you lost what little sense the Lord blessed you with." Mother Porter shook her head. "There's enough trouble in this world. Don't know why you feel the need to go out of your way lookin' for more."

While Randy knew he took risks, he did not

indiscriminately ignore the color barriers that had been established before he was born. He weighed the pros and cons before crossing lines. And, though things did not always turn out the way he expected, there were times, like meeting Cass, when the outcome was better than he had hoped.

"Sometimes I can't help myself," he replied, brushing his fingertips across Cass's jawline.

"Don't know why I waste my time worryin' on grown folks." Despite her statement, the worry lines creasing his mother-in-law's forehead did not fade. "I got dinner to fix," she announced. She reached behind and grabbed Sylvia's hand.

Randy stepped to the side and pulled Cass with him to make room for the older woman to pass.

"I'll be there in a minute, Momma."

"No, visit with your husband." She called over her shoulder, "Avery, come help me, and let the adults catch up."

"But I wanna stay with my daddy." The girl poked out her bottom lip.

"Girl, what did I say?" Mother Porter's tone said she was not going to let her granddaughter get away with talking back to her.

"Why don't you go make something special for your old man?" Joe Frank's baritone voice softened. "I'll still be here when you get back." He ruffled her hair.

The girl's smile returned. She stood on the tips of her toes and kissed her father's cheek before skipping out of the house.

Mother Porter pointed Sylvia and Joe Frank's youngest toward the door. Shara shifted in her grandmother's arms. She stared over the woman's shoulder at Randy, appearing ready to take flight in the event he made a move toward them.

Cass's shoulders drooped under his arm. Randy picked up his coat and draped it around her. "Come with me." He took her hand, not giving her much choice but to follow him.

Behind them, his father-in-law and eldest brother-in-law tossed one question after another at Joe Frank. Their deep voices did not drown out the rapid commands Mother Porter tossed at her young helpers in the kitchen.

Randy led Cass to the hickory tree that hovered over the house like an overprotective mother watching after her children. He leaned against the trunk, slipped his hands underneath the coat, and pulled her to him. To his right, a soft breeze stirred the dirt in the bare field, which was enjoying a well-deserved rest after providing a plentiful harvest a month earlier.

After being reassured the draft notice had not been sent in error, Randy had suggested Cass move to North Carolina to be near her family when she gave birth to the baby they not long before had discovered had been conceived. Though she would have to give up some conveniences, like electricity, indoor plumbing, and the corner grocery store, the tranquility of the farm more than made up for what it lacked.

"This is not the homecoming I wanted for you," Cass said, fingering the short hairs at his nape. "The girls won't go near you. None of your favorite dishes are prepared. There's nothing here for you."

"That's not true." He wished Sylvia and Shara could show a quarter of the enthusiasm Avery had showed her father. And he also craved a meal that was prepared with love. However, the woman whose image had gotten him through more than eight hundred lonely nights was there with him. "I missed you so much," he whispered before he lowered his lips to hers.

Cass parted her lips as she pressed closer to him, silently conveying how much she missed him. She tasted of chocolate; a sign that she had sampled the frosting on her mother's cake when no one was looking.

The evidence Cass had not lost the playful side he had grown to love was reassuring. Though he had received regular letters insisting everything was fine, he had worried how much was true and how much was invented to keep him from worrying.

Cass's tongue teased his until he felt a familiar stir in his pants. What was supposed to reassure her of what mattered most to him was getting out of hand. He needed to pull back before he lost control and pulled her to the barn. But no matter how loud his brain screamed for him to release her, his body would not comply.

His fingers wanted to caress her soft skin. His lips wanted to kiss every inch of her. And his ears wanted to ring from her groans.

Forget the barn. Randy wanted to spin Cass around, press her against the tree and demonstrate his desire for his wife before God, his in-laws, and anyone else who happened by.

Without considering the cons of his plan, Randy pushed away from the tree. As he tightened his hold on Cass, a voice called from the house, "Hey, Randy, whatever happened to that soldier with the hairy ass?"

"Joseph Franklin Porter, you watch your mouth!"

Mother Porter scolded.

"Sorry."

Randy pulled back from Cass and glared at his brother-in-law, who leaned out his parent's bedroom window. There was nothing contrite about the smirk on the man's face, leading Randy to believe Joe Frank's choice of words was deliberate.

The man's scheme worked. The image of his bunkmate successfully quashed Randy's desire. In fact, he feared it might have affected his future ability to rise to the occasion.

Chapter 3

"You should head back to Norfolk tonight," her mother announced as Cass stepped into the kitchen, balancing a stack of plates in her hands.

"But I don't have to be back at work 'til Monday." She placed the dishes on the shelf next to the washbasin.

"That'll give you three days to get reacquainted with your husband." The lantern that hung from a hook on the wall illuminated the woman's face. The glint in her eye said she was aware of how Randy and Cass had carried on by the tree.

Cass's face warmed. With two children, it was no secret Randy and she had enjoyed each other's company on more than one occasion. However, growing up, there was never a discussion about what transpired between men and women. It wasn't until her first marriage that she learned what went where. The lesson had been unpleasant, and it wasn't until her relationship with Randy that she had learned to enjoy the experience. She, therefore, did not feel comfortable discussing her relationship with her mother, no matter how innocently the woman phrased her statement.

"I guess we can use the time to help the girls get used to their father," Cass said, attempting to steer the conversation to a topic she found more comfortable.

"No, the girls'll stay here." Her mother nodded at

the children sitting at the table, devouring slices of cake. "Make this weekend about Randy and you. Once you take the girls, it'll be hard for y'all to find time for each other."

If anyone should know about how hard it could get, it would be her mother. With six children running around the house, it couldn't have been easy for her parents to find a quiet moment for them to be together.

Still, Cass felt guilty leaving the girls behind. It was one thing for her parents to watch the children while she was working; it was another to leave the girls so Randy and she could be alone.

"But you'll have Avery and June," she said, remembering her mother had made the same offer to Martha Lynn when they learned Joe Frank was coming home.

"I can handle four girls for a couple of days." Her mother placed a damp hand on Cass's arm. "I raised five boys, and with you chasin' after them, it sometimes felt like I had seven." Her mother nudged Cass toward the door. "Go get your things."

Her mother raised an eyebrow, silently warning her to save her breath. The woman had made up her mind, and there was no argument Cass could make that would change it.

Cass had to admit she liked the idea of a few days alone with Randy. After she was born, Sylvia had demanded so much time and attention the only thing Randy and Cass had the energy to do when they climbed into bed was sleep. With the two girls, there would be more demands.

She finally conceded by returning to the house and heading to the bedroom her brothers had shared when they were growing up. After transferring a few clothes Randy had left behind from the trunk in the corner into the duffel bag he had dropped by the door, she grabbed the bag she had not bothered to unpack when she arrived the previous night.

"Where you heading off to?" Joe Frank asked as she walked into the living room carrying the two bags. "Joining the Army?"

"You're so not funny," Cass replied.

Randy rose from one of the ladderback chairs they had brought in from the front porch to accommodate the extra company that stopped by to celebrate. "What's goin' on?" he asked, taking the bags from her.

"Momma offered to watch the girls while we go to Norfolk."

He glanced toward the back door, where her mother stood. "Are you sure?"

"I'm tired of y'all actin' like I don't know my own mind." She crossed her arms over the apron covering her chest, signaling her patience was running thin.

"I meant, thank you." Randy walked over to his mother-in-law and kissed her cheek. "I appreciate the offer."

As he pulled back, Shara peeked from behind her grandmother. She stared at her father for a heartbeat before ducking back to the safety of the kitchen.

"Patience." Cass's mother patted his arm. "They'll come around."

He forced a smile onto his face as he relinquished his position to Cass.

"Don't spend all your time frettin' over them." Her mother embraced her. "Enjoy the time with your man."

Cass kissed her mother's cheek. "Thanks again,

Momma."

"You two get." Her mother glanced at Joe Frank, who was perched on the edge of the couch, eating his third slice of cake. "You should take your wife and go, too."

Martha Lynn jumped from her seat by the window. "But don't you need help cleaning up...moving the furniture?" Her gaze darted to the table Cass had cleared while Randy and Joe Frank told tales about the service, with Martha Lynn listening as though there was nothing else to do.

She wrung her hands like an anxious bride. However, unlike Cass, Martha Lynn had known what to expect on her wedding night, for it was the celebration before the vows that had forced her to stand before a preacher.

Deciding she would rather hit the road than worry about her sister-in-law, Cass stepped around her mother, onto the back porch. She waved Sylvia and Shara forward and kissed both girls. After eliciting promises of good reports from them, she walked around to the front of the house, where Randy was talking to Joe Frank.

"What am I thinking?" she mumbled.

"What's wrong?" Randy asked.

"I forgot something."

"The keys?"

"Okay, I forgot two things," she called over her shoulder as she rushed up the steps and through the front door. "Brother, the keys," she yelled to Mack, Jr. before she ducked into the bedroom and grabbed the case sitting by the door.

Her eldest sibling, who had driven to Rocky Mount

and brought Joe Frank and Randy back to the farm, dug the keys from his pants pocket and tossed them across the room as she emerged from the bedroom. With the skill obtained from being the only girl in a family with five boys, she caught the keys without slowing her step.

"Got 'em." She dangled the keys in the air as she emerged from the house.

"I'll be finished in a sec," Randy called from the back seat, where he was placing the bags.

Cass sprinted to the driver's side, opened the door, and slid the case onto the floor behind the seat. She tossed her coat on the back seat, then climbed behind the wheel and started the engine. Once she had adjusted the mirrors, she glanced to the passenger side, where Randy leaned in and stared at her.

****

Growing up, Cass had to rely on her two feet to get from one location to the next. When a trip to town required help getting the purchases back home, the family utilized the mule and wagon. Therefore, it had taken Cass a while to get used to riding in cars.

To return home and have her not only climb behind the wheel but adjust the mirrors like she had been driving for years left Randy speechless.

"Did you want to drive?" she asked, breaking the minute-long silence.

He climbed into the car and closed the door. "No, it's just…how…why…when did you learn how to drive?" He tried to recall if she had mentioned the acquired skill in her weekly letters.

"Brother took me out about a week after you left." She made a smooth U-turn that would impress a seasoned driver. "Momma wanted me to do something other than sit around and mope for you." She glanced over her shoulder and waved to the girls who stood on the porch. "The skill came in handy when I decided to find work in Norfolk."

Randy settled back as she faced forward and drove from the farm.

With her left hand on the steering wheel, she maneuvered down the two-lane road with only the headlights to guide the way. She patted his leg with her free hand.

How could their roles have reversed? He used to give her the reassuring pat whenever they went for a drive.

A pit settled in his stomach. Despite his eagerness to return home and pick up where they had left off, his intuition told him things had changed. He was not sure if the changes would be for the better or for worse.

Randy pushed aside his apprehensions. The conversation during the two-hour drive to Norfolk was light, with Cass offering him a slew of anecdotes about the children and him telling her about life in the service.

"What's California like?" she asked.

"Didn't see much of it," he replied.

"Why not? Surely they gave you a chance to see the sights?"

"The sights the other men wanted to see were not on my itinerary."

Randy recalled the cribs the men, single and married, would brag about visiting when they were on leave. Though he missed the warmth of a female surrounding him and the soft touch caressing his skin, he knew it would not be the same without the emotional attachment he had with Cass. Therefore, when his physical needs demanded attention, he would find a private corner and take matters into his own hand.

"Maybe we can go back and visit it together," Randy suggested.

"We may have to put that dream on hold for another sixteen years," Cass said.

"It'll be worth the wait."

Cass stopped at a corner and waited for a couple to cross the street. Despite the holiday, the sidewalks were filled with people dressed in their best, wandering in and out of venues that offered everything from dance floors where they could work up a sweat to performances they could simply sit back and enjoy. The area reminded Randy of the U-Street District in Washington, D.C., where they had settled after they were married.

"The majority of the businesses in this area are owned by coloreds," she said, confirming his suspicions as she continued up the street.

The thriving neighborhood had him looking forward to seeing the apartment she had shared with Martha Lynn. He hoped she had been able to get a good deal on the rent.

Cass turned a right onto East Princess Anne Road. As they continued east, his apprehension grew. The distance between the houses became wider, and the dwellings were more primitive. While he could live without some conveniences when he was on the farm, there were certain amenities, like electricity and his closest neighbor being less than a mile from him, he insisted on when he resided in the city.

He peered at the gauge when Cass pulled into a gas station. Before he could point out that the needle still sat equally between the F and E, she drove past the pumps.

"What is this place?" Randy asked as she drove around to the back of the store.

"Home away from home," Cass replied, parking next to a set of steps leading to the upper level. "Martha Lynn and I shared the top floor. Our landlord lives on the first floor with his grandson."

A chill ran down Randy's spine as he stared at the woods beyond the two-story structure. It was no place for two women to reside by themselves. At least on the farm her father had the shotgun hanging over the front door, and both her parents knew how to use the weapon.

Randy knew nothing about the man who lived in the apartment beneath his wife. Besides the obvious questions about the man's background and character, what could he do to protect her if someone with lecherous intentions came around?

He decided not to dwell on the matter. It was not like Cass would be there by herself anymore. He was home for good and, in a few days, would move her to a more populated area.

With his mind made up about the living arrangements, Randy climbed out of the car and grabbed the bags from the back. He followed Cass, who had already ascended the steps and unlocked a door.

Randy stepped into the apartment as Cass reached over the table in the center of the room and pulled the string to the light fixture. The single bulb flickered on, offering barely more light than the moon.

Randy's pressure rose as he scanned his surroundings. The kitchen to his left was smaller than

Mother Porter's, and it housed an icebox and a wood-burning stove that had to have been installed when the building was erected at the turn of the century. To his right, a shabby sofa sat under the window next to a side table with chipped blue paint.

Randy silently cursed the government for ripping him away from his family. He should have been home, providing for his wife and children so they could have a house of their own, not making do at his in-laws' farm or in a hovel over a gas station.

Cass reached past him and pushed the door closed. Though he had vowed not to make an issue of the place that evening, he could not hold his tongue after viewing the interior.

Randy opened his mouth to list the reasons they would not be spending the night there, but before he uttered the first syllable, Cass pressed her lips against his and stroked his tongue with hers. She was no longer the shy, naïve woman he'd met years ago. She was a confident woman who went after what she wanted, and to his delight, she wanted him.

He became hard so fast his head spun. They had made love only hours before he left for the service so he could take the memory of her with him. But the memories had been a poor substitute for the real person. He could not feel her body writhing beneath his, savor her sweet kisses or hear her soft cries before she came.

Randy dropped the bags at his feet and reached for Cass. Instead of coming to him, she pulled back and pushed his coat off his shoulders.

"What's the rush?" he gasped, trying to catch his breath.

"I want you in me before I wake up," she replied,

clawing at the buttons on his shirt.

Randy understood the sentiment. Too many mornings he had awakened from dreams so real he'd reached for her, hoping to enjoy one more kiss before he was forced to roll out of bed. It was only after he caressed the air that he would open his eyes to the disappointing view of the sagging bunk over him.

Cass abandoned the last three buttons and started unbuckling his belt. Anxious to feel her surrounding him, Randy pushed her skirt up to her waist and pushed down the silk she wore underneath until it slid to the floor. He lifted her up as his own pants cleared his hips.

She wrapped her legs around his waist while he guided himself into her. Her head dropped to one shoulder, and she held on tight to the other. Tears of joy filled his eyes as her soft groans reached his ears.

Having achieved his goal, Randy wanted to relish the moment. Careful not to trip over the pants sliding to his knees or, more importantly, slip out of paradise, he shuffled the ten steps to the table. He perched her on the end and prayed the furniture supported their weight.

Though he had all night and the next day and every day after that, Randy was in no hurry to finish. He pulled her sweater off her and dropped it onto the floor. Knowing Cass would have a word or two to say about any ruined material, he resisted the temptation to yank open her dress. Instead, he carefully pushed each fabric-covered button through its hole until he could peel off her top without tearing it.

Cass reached behind her and unhooked her bra. As the material slid away from her body, Randy leaned down and latched onto a nipple. His left hand kneaded the unattended breast.

"I missed you."

Randy could not bring himself to release Cass in order to echo her sentiment. He grunted his words of endearment around her breast, hoping his actions spoke for themselves.

Cass writhed beneath him until he could no longer remain still. He pulled his mouth from her breast and wrapped his arms around her. His hips moved against her, pressing deep into her.

His brain screamed for him to slow down. He could not ruin their first time together by reaching his peak before she reached hers. Her squirming did not help matters, and he felt the pressure in his groin.

Just as his body could no longer hold back, Cass tightened her grip on him. Her short nails dug into his shoulders, and her body trembled against his.

Randy's legs shook as his body found release. His heart slammed against his chest to the same beat as Cass's. Bright lights clouded his vision, while their panting filled the air.

He braced himself against the table to keep from falling to the ground. As his vision cleared, he glanced down at the woman smiling up at him.

Strands of her hair stood out from her head, sweat covered her brow, and the clothes she still wore were disheveled. Yet she was the most beautiful sight he had ever seen.

Randy kissed Cass, deeply and thoroughly, until self-preservation forced them apart.

"Don't you want to see the rest of the apartment?" Cass gasped, running a finger down his hip.

Liking the way she thought, he wrapped his arms around her and picked her off the table as he straightened. "How 'bout we start in the bedroom," he suggested, shuffling across the room.

Chapter 4

Randy woke with the sigh of a man whose wife had caressed every inch of his body before she allowed him to drift off to sleep. If that was the welcome home he could expect after an extended absence, he would consider enlisting for another two years. On second thought, he would rather wake Cass for an encore performance.

He rolled onto his back and blindly reached for his wife. His heart slammed against his chest when his hand felt air. Had it all been a dream? When he opened his eyes, would he still be in the barracks, craving the touch of the woman he'd married?

Outside, a driver beeped his horn before he shut off an engine that rattled so hard the windows vibrated. A gruff voice called over the squealing door hinges for the customer to keep his britches on.

Randy cracked open an eye. To his relief, he was not lying in a dreary room with three other men. Instead, he was alone in a full-sized bed in a hovel located on the edge of civilization.

"Cass," he called out, despite the silence that filled the apartment.

He considered going back to sleep with the hope that she would have returned when he woke again, yet his bladder had other ideas.

With a groan, he tossed aside the patchwork quilt

Mother Porter had made from Cass's childhood dresses and swung his legs over the side of the bed. He wiggled his toes against the multi-colored braided rug, grateful for something other than the bare floor underneath his feet. The clothes he had strewn over the floor the previous night lay neatly folded on the edge of the four-drawer dresser that sat behind the lone closet.

Randy was tempted to head to the bathroom in the buff, but despite the thick green curtains covering the window, a breeze drifting through the cracks chilled the room. With a sigh, he pulled on his boxers and undershirt.

Once he was as dressed as he planned to get that day, he shuffled into the bathroom and relieved himself. When he depressed the handle on the toilet, the water receded so slowly he wondered if the little liquid he had added to the bowl had stopped up the plumbing.

After the water finally flushed, he shuffled to the sink by the door and turned on the hot water. The pipes clanged with such force he feared the sink would break loose and fly across the room. Rusty water spurted out of the faucet, staining the white porcelain bowl.

In the five minutes he had been awake, the place had done little to redeem itself. Instead, it made him more determined to speak to Cass about their options before the end of the day.

By the time he had finished calculating how long it would take them to pack, the water was running clear. Randy grabbed the soap and stuck his hand under the faucet. He shivered as the cold water ran over his appendages.

He knew he should at least be grateful to have indoor plumbing. If they had stayed at his parents-in-law's house, he would have to draw the water from the well before he could perform the task of washing his hands.

As he worked the soap into a lather, the water spurted a second time. A burst of steam spilled from the faucet and scalding water poured over his hands.

"Motherf—"

Randy jumped back and dropped the soap. It slid across the floor and underneath the clawfoot tub. With a growl, he turned off the water, snatched a damp washcloth from a rack on the wall behind him and walked out of the bathroom. He would retrieve the soap later, or better yet, let the next tenants deal with it when they moved in.

He wrapped the cloth around his throbbing hand as he surveyed the front room for the second time. It was not hard to recognize the little touches Cass had added to make the temporary living quarters feel more like home. An orange-and-cream-colored crocheted doily covered the top of the side table, and matching mats covered the back and arms of the sofa. Dark orange curtains were tied back from the window, allowing the sun to light up the room.

The suitcases he had carried in the previous night sat by the door, with the clothes he had peeled off Cass folded on top. His focus turned to the case Cass had set on the table before she deserted him that morning.

Randy stroked the smooth black leather that protected the saxophone that had once belonged to his mentor. Before he was drafted, he had never gone more than three days without touching the instrument. After two years of neglect, he was anxious about the condition the instrument would be in.

His hands shook as he unbuckled the brass latches and opened the top. With the same care he'd used when he held Sylvia for the first time, Randy lifted the saxophone from its velvet cushion. He examined the instrument, which looked as if it had been polished that morning. His eyes misted over at the lengths Cass had gone to in caring for his treasured possession.

Ignoring the throbbing in the back of his hand, Randy assembled the saxophone, then closed his eyes and placed the reed to his lip. He played the first verse of "Ain't Nobody's Business," which Cass and he had decided to add to their act the day he received his draft notice. Though the instrument was out of tune, the music awakened the memories of their performances. Onstage, for the duration of each song, it was only the two of them performing for each other.

Randy remained blissfully lost in thought until a fist slammed against the front door.

"Martha Lynn Porter," the gruff voice from below called out. "I've warned you about that noise."

Randy abruptly stopped playing. He walked over and snatched open the door as the visitor's fist flew forward. The stranger's dark eyes narrowed, his broad nostril's flared, and his lips were twisted in rage.

"May I help you?" Randy asked. The brisk November air raised goosebumps on every inch of exposed skin.

"What the—" The man's eyes widened, and his mouth dropped open. "Well, I'll be. Girl done crossed over," the man mumbled, taking in Randy's rumpled hair and lack of clothing. He gawked for a minute before he squared his shoulders as if he suddenly remembered the purpose of his visit. "Where's Martha

Lynn?"

"Last I saw her, she was in Piney Woods with her husband."

The tick in the man's jaw was slight, yet prominent enough to alert Randy that the man did not appreciate the wiseass reply. "Who are you?"

Before Randy could debate the pros and cons of mouthing off to the man who was four to six inches taller and slightly bulkier, a voice muttered, "Uh-oh."

He glanced past the man at Cass, who stood at the foot of the stairs. The heartbeat it took before anyone said a word felt like an eternity.

"Hell, Cass?" The man's tone rose. A glint of disappointment shone in his eyes, indicating the conclusion that had settled in his mind.

"Mr. Johnston, it's not what you think. This is my husband."

"Your what?" The man's head continuously turned from one person to the other until Randy was sure the man would get dizzy and fall the twelve feet to the ground. "I thought he was still servin'."

Cass ascended the stairs and stepped in front of Randy. "He surprised me at my parents' yesterday." She peered over her shoulder. "Randy, this is Albert Johnston, our landlord."

Randy held out his hand to the man and waited. How someone responded to the gesture told Randy a lot about the person. Avoidance said the person would not tolerate his presence. A glance of a palm against his spoke of someone who wanted to appear accepting, yet deep down had no desire to meet him. And a firm grasp said the person was willing to give him a chance before passing judgment.

Despite his obvious shock, the man grasped Randy's hand and gave it a hearty shake. "Cass talked about you all the time...though she left out a detail or two."

Randy tried to maintain the smile on his face, despite the sting of the statement. They had been together six years and had two children. So why did she hide their relationship?

Instead of broaching the subject with words or a glance, Randy said, "Sorry about the noise." He released the man's hand and stroked the saxophone hanging from his neck. "I guess I wasn't thinkin', in the excitement of bein' back."

"Understandable. Just get that thing tuned." Mr. Johnston peered down at Cass. "If you don't mind, I'd like a word with you."

"Anythin' you need to discuss with her, you can discuss with both of us," Randy insisted.

"No." Cass shoved the brown paper shopping bag from her arms into his free hand. "I'll talk with Mr. Johnston while you take this into the house."

Randy frowned. Instead of backing down, she placed her hands on his shoulders and gently pushed him back.

"And while you're at it, put some clothes on," she added before she pulled the door closed.

****

Cass turned to face the man who had equally watched over her and fussed at Martha Lynn during the twelve months they had been renting the apartment from him. While her sister-in-law had taken an instant dislike to him, suspecting he would be in their business, Cass liked him for the same reason. She felt safe in the apartment, knowing he was keeping tabs on who lurked outside.

"Don't have to worry about a man pushin' you around." His eyes twinkled with amusement.

"Learned to speak up after my first marriage."

Cass was embarrassed to think about the years she'd wasted being a devoted wife to a man who insisted on finding relief in the beds of other women while failing to provide shelter and food for the woman he'd married. Had any children been conceived during their time together, they might have grown up thinking it was all right for men to treat women like dirt and a woman had no choice but to take what was dished out to her.

"Speakin' of marriages, why didn't you tell me?" Mr. Johnston asked.

"Wasn't sure how you'd react," she confessed.

Randy and she had had many encounters with people who had opinions about them being together. Even when they were just friends, people made comments and tried to keep them apart.

"I won't lie and say it don't concern me. People find out, and there's bound to be trouble."

"Does that mean you want us to leave?"

She could not hide the disappointment in her voice. The apartment was not the White House, yet it was comfortable enough, and at six dollars a week, the rent was just right.

"Considerin' *you* never gave me any problems, I'm willin' to let you stay." He started down the stairs, stopped midway down, and turned back to her. "You need to understand, though, if there's trouble, I can't help you."

"Randy and I wouldn't ask you to." When they made the choice to be together, they did not expect others to fight their fights.

With a nod, he continued down the steps. Once he turned the corner, she retreated into the apartment.

Randy stood at the table, dissembling his saxophone. His posture became rigid when she stopped next to him, removed her coat, and draped it over the back of a chair.

"You plan on walking around the house half-dressed all day?" She moved the shopping bag from the table and set it on top of the cabinet pushed against the wall between stove and sink.

"I wasn't plannin' on gettin' dressed at all," he mumbled. "But I woke up in bed alone."

"We needed food." She pulled a dozen eggs from the bag. "I only purchased enough for two days when I went to the market on Monday." She placed the carton in the icebox. "I wasn't planning on returning 'til Sunday."

"Guess I kinda put a damper on your plans."

She froze with a bag of lima beans in her hand. "What's that supposed to mean?" She crossed her arms over her chest and leaned against the sink. Though he had stopped fiddling with his saxophone, he had not faced her.

"How long did you plan on hidin' me?"

It took a heartbeat before she comprehended and another second for the shock to fade enough for her to reply.

"I wasn't hiding anything. I just didn't mention that my husband was white."

"Why not?"

What had he expected from her? To shout it from the top of the tallest building in the city? And, in case someone failed to hear the announcement, stop every person she passed on the street and inform them?

"Tell me, what did your Army buddies say when you told them your wife's colored?"

His shoulders slumped like a ball that had been punctured with a needle.

"I thought so." She tossed the beans on top of the cabinet and walked over to him. "Randy, I'm not ashamed of you." She stroked his shoulder. "I thought I proved that last night."

He turned to her. His head hung low, but she did not miss the shame in his eyes.

"You're right." He sighed. "I didn't go into details about our marriage. Hell, I didn't even tell them I had children."

While others would be hurt by the disclosure, Cass understood his need to keep some information to himself. There was no telling who would object to him being married to a colored woman nor how they would express their displeasure.

"As for last night"—he pulled her to him until there was no doubt that he was not totally spent—"you more than proved how much you like me." He stroked her cheek with his cloth-wrapped hand.

Cass took his hand and slowly peeled back the cloth. "What happened to you?"

"Water burnt me."

"Crap, I forgot to warn you about the water," she muttered, examining the red skin. "You have to wait until after the water spurts out a second time, then adjust the temperature."

"I kinda figured as much."

"What did you put on this?"

"Nothin'. I got distracted." He nodded toward the case.

She grabbed his wrist and pulled him to the kitchen sink. "You should've put something on this right away." She turned on the faucet.

"Don't you think it's too late for that?"

"Humor me," she said, shoving his hand under the cold water before she ran out of the room. Less than a minute later, she returned with the tip of an Aloe Vera spike. After another minute, she turned off the water, patted his hand dry, and squeezed onto it the soothing gel from the plant.

"We need to get outta here," he said as she gently massaged the gel into the back of his hand. "We can't live like this."

"But Mr. Johnston said we could stay."

"Probably 'cause he's afraid he won't be able to rent this hellhole to someone else."

She raised her head and frowned. "This place isn't that bad."

"Honey, I've lived in dumps better than this. There's a breeze comin' through the cracks around the window—"

"Something you wouldn't feel if you put some clothes on," she mumbled as she squeezed more gel onto his hand.

He rolled his eyes and continued, "These appliances were here when Lincoln was President. The pipes rattle, and the faucets spit out brown water…and that's when they're not tryin' to scald a person to death."

"This place is only a thirty-minute walk to my job." Cass raised one finger. "The rent's decent." She raised a second finger. "And Mr. Johnston always kept an eye out for me." A third finger popped up. "I can keep on, but I'm eventually going to run out of fingers."

"But this isn't the type of place for you." He wrapped his arms around her waist. "Cass, you're too good for...for this." He waved his good hand at the space. "For chrissakes, you used to headline shows."

"But I'm not doing that at this moment." She reached up and lowered his arm back to her waist. "Right now, I'm a mother trying to take care of my babies until my husband's capable of providing for them."

Randy flinched, and Cass knew her comment had hit a nerve. He had never known his father, and his mother had been more interested in finding her next man than taking care of her child. Cass, therefore, knew how important it was to Randy that he do better by his children.

"You just got back yesterday." She stroked his arm. "Can't we stay here till you find a job and we're ready to bring the girls up here?"

One second passed, then another and another. After the fourth tick from the clock in the living room, she suspected they would have their second argument before the end of the day.

Cass was aware the apartment was not a mansion; Martha Lynn had reminded her daily of the downfalls of the dwelling. However, she could not see why it mattered so much to Randy. Shouldn't it have been enough that they were together?

A minute passed before he nodded his head. "Fine,

just don't get too comfortable. I intend to get you outta here soon." He leaned forward and nibbled her earlobe.

Cass hated arguing with Randy, but she sure enjoyed reconciling with him. Her body molded against him, and his excitement pressed against her hip.

"I take it you're not putting more clothes on anytime soon?"

He shook his head.

"And mine are about to be removed?"

He nodded before tossing her over his shoulder.

Cass laughed as he carried her toward the bedroom. There were so many things they still needed to work out, but she figured she would take her mother's advice and enjoy her time with her husband. Before they knew it, tomorrow would come, and they would have more than a few worries to deal with.

Chapter 5

Randy growled as his arm dropped onto the empty mattress next to him. He was tired of waking to find his wife missing.

Yes, it was nice to wake up with the aroma of bacon filling the house. But with all the mornings of waking up by himself, he had vowed that after he returned home, he would never be alone again.

He rolled out of bed, pulled on a pair of boxers, and shuffled to the bathroom. By Friday night, he had learned to appreciate the bathtub that was large enough for two adults to indulge in a leisurely bubble bath…amongst other things.

A smile tugged at Randy's lips as he recalled the numerous times he'd made love to his wife. The only room they had not ventured into had belonged to Martha Lynn. Cass had wanted to clean the bedroom, though he was unsure why. The two of them were able to live in one room until he made other arrangements for them.

After he finished answering Mother Nature's morning call, he washed his hands before strolling into the kitchen. He figured a hearty meal would hit the spot, before they hit the bed again. Of course, depending on how impatient Cass was, they might not get away from the table.

"'Bout time you woke, sleepyhead," Cass said,

carrying a cast iron pot to the table.

Randy stopped short and gawked at the woman. A pair of dungarees and a beige flannel shirt had replaced the modest dress she usually wore around the house. A blue bandanna was wrapped around her thick hair, while a pair of work boots covered her feet.

Although he did not expect her to prance around the house in satin and silk, the outfit was a far cry from the gowns she had worn when she performed in clubs.

"What's with the get-up?"

She glanced up from the grits she had been spooning into the single bowl on the table. "This is what I wear to work," she replied.

It dawned on Randy that they had never discussed her job. "What's the name of the play?" he asked, recalling her desire to try her hand at acting.

"I'm not in a play. I work down by the shipyard."

Randy wracked his brain to figure out what she could possibly be doing at the shipyard. Nothing about her outfit made her stand out as someone who entertained the troops—worked beside them, maybe, but entertain them? Never.

His stomach turned as the realization dawned on him. From the correspondences some of the other soldiers in his unit had received, he'd been aware that jobs vacated by men who were drafted were being filled by women. He just never thought his wife would become a Rosie.

"Hell, no."

Cass jumped at his outburst. "What's gotten into you?"

"No wife of mine's workin' in a factory."

"That's good, 'cause I'm workin' in the shipyard,

not a factory." She returned to the stove and exchanged the pot for a plate overflowing with bacon, eggs, and toast.

"I'm not jokin', Cass. You're quittin'."

She chuckled. "Of course I am." She set the plate next to the bowl, then crossed her arms over her chest and glared at him. "Once you get a job." Her tone was devoid of humor.

"No, you're quittin' now."

How could her life veer so far off the path she had been on? People used to pack clubs to hear her sing. Now she was laboring in a shipyard. Wasn't her career supposed to go forward, not back?

"And what do you expect us to live on? The twenty dollars the government's going to send you each week?"

As frugal as Cass was, the family of four would have no problem surviving on the benefit…if he had any intention of applying for it.

During his discharge, he had been given a brief explanation of the benefits he could apply for in order to help him adjust to civilian life. However, expecting he would have no problems finding a job, he'd merely thanked the lieutenant for the information before shoving his paperwork into his bag.

"What happened to the money we saved?"

"It's in the bank, and we're not touching it as long as one of us is capable of bringing in a paycheck. How long do you expect that to last if neither one of us is working?"

He did not expect either one of them to be out of work long enough for them to blow through the savings. Since getting his first job at the age of ten, he had not been unemployed more than a week.

"I don't like it," he grumbled.

"Why are you suddenly against me working?"

"'Cause it's a man's job."

"Would you feel better if I quit that and scrub floors?"

Randy was surprised his head did not explode at the suggestion. That was not a question that should spill from her mouth.

While any job was more respectable than mooching off family or allowing their children to go hungry, he would not hear of her cleaning houses. She had been a headliner, singing in New York and D.C.

"Couldn't you find somethin' in a club?"

"There's only a handful of clubs for coloreds down here. The ones that are paying something already have their talent. The others couldn't afford to give me half of what I'm making at the shipyard." She glanced at her watch. "Listen, I've got to go. We'll discuss this when I get home tonight."

She grabbed a metal lunchbox, gave him a peck on the cheek, and rushed out the door before he could continue the argument.

Randy stared at the food purchased with the money his wife made doing a job he was supposed to be doing. His stomach turned. While some men had no problem living off their wives, he was not one of them.

Unable to stomach the cuisine made by his woman before she rushed out to support him, Randy covered the plates and placed them in the icebox. He then headed to the bathroom to get ready to start his day.

****

"You're too happy today," Bertha Grover yelled

over the lunch whistle. She set the drill she had been using onto the cart that held the tools they needed to repair the stern of the ship. "What gives?"

"Don't you remember?" Doreen Matthews asked, tossing the woman the rag she used to wipe oil from her hands. "Cass's brother returned and took Martha Lynn off her hands."

"Come to think of it, it has been quiet around here today." Bertha barely brushed the rag over her hands before she tossed it on top of the drill. "Please thank your brother for takin' his wife and her whinin' away from here."

"Better yet, I'll make a cake for you to take to him next weekend," Doreen added. "It's the least I could do to show my gratitude."

"She wasn't that bad," Cass protested.

Bertha placed her lunchbox on her lap and crossed her arms over her flat chest. "Girl complained so much, I volunteered to clean the toilets just to get away from her."

Doreen placed her hands on her hips. In a high-pitched tone that did not come close to sounding like Martha Lynn, she whined, "I'm hot."

"I'm thirsty," Bertha chimed in.

"I'm tired," the two women whined in unison.

Cass grabbed her lunchbox off the bottom shelf of the cart. "You should be ashamed of yourselves, mocking her behind her back."

"Now, you know we're just having a little fun." Doreen draped an arm over Cass's shoulders. "We meant nothing by it."

Bertha snorted. "Speak for yourself." She unfolded her arms to unlatch her lunchbox and toss back the lid.

"I meant every word I said, and I wasn't afraid to tell her to her face."

To Cass's dismay, the woman spoke the truth. A week did not go by without Martha Lynn and Bertha arguing after the latter would tell the former to cease her complaining.

Cass knew better than most how her sister-in-law could get under someone's skin. In addition to working beside Martha Lynn eight hours a day, five days a week, she spent twice that amount of time in an apartment with the woman. Still, she felt like she would be betraying Joe Frank if she did not defend his wife.

"Let's talk about something else," she suggested, opening her lunchbox.

Though there was a cafeteria where they could spread out, the three women preferred their dusty workstation to the dark corner management had set aside in the lunchroom for the colored employees.

"You were telling us why you're all smiles," Doreen said around her turkey sandwich.

"Just happy my brother got home safely."

Cass felt a twinge of guilt telling the lie. She wanted to reveal the real reason she was ready to break out into song, but she could not take the risk. If she told the women Randy had returned, they would insist on meeting him. And she didn't want to deal with the possible fallout.

There was the chance neither of them would give a fig about the color of Randy's skin. But there was also the possibility one or both of them would disapprove and cause enough trouble to get Cass fired. Until Randy was in a position to support them, she wanted to hold onto the job.

"Uh-oh, someone's going home," Doreen muttered.

Since the end of the war, returning soldiers had been showing up at the shipyard to take their wives back home. Some quietly approached the foreman to inform him that the woman would no longer return to her duties. Others inquired about taking their woman's place on the payroll. And then there were the few who made a show of dragging their wives out, to let everyone know who truly wore the pants in the relationship.

Cass unwrapped her ham sandwich and bit off a piece. She glanced across the floor and nearly choked at the sight of Randy talking to her foreman. Surely the man was not crazy enough to march in there and demand she quit her job. Aside from their need of the income, the public acknowledgement of their relationship could be potentially dangerous.

A high-pitched squeal preceded the teeth-clenching shrill of gears grinding metal. The foreman patted Randy's shoulder before rushing off to inspect the latest calamity.

Having seen the foreman's "I wish you the best of luck" pat on more than one occasion, Cass suspected Randy had not revealed his connection to her but only inquired about a position at the shipyard.

Randy lingered by the door as he scanned the room. Cass held her breath as his gaze moved past the small clusters of colored women enjoying their lunch at their workstations and the few white women completing tasks before they retreated to the cafeteria.

His emotionless mask made it impossible to read his thoughts. However, the slightest glance from him would alert everyone to their relationship.

Cass released the breath when his gaze moved past her, lingering no longer than it did on the other women in the room. Once he took in the entire area, he lit a cigarette and strolled out.

"Nah, just another ex-soldier looking for work." Bertha bit into an apple, showering Cass's arm with bits of juice.

"They need to post a sign, White Men Need Not Apply," Doreen added. "It would save these guys some time."

****

"Why were you down at the shipyard?" Cass asked, stepping into the apartment.

Randy glanced up from the newspaper spread out in front of him. A copy of the morning edition peeped from underneath.

His chair scraped across the floor as he pushed back from the table. "Figured I'd make a trade." He met her at the door and kissed her forehead. "My skills for my wife's."

"You could've asked me and saved yourself a trip." She pushed the door closed. "Other soldiers have tried, but as long as they've got women and coloreds willing to take less than what a white man would expect, they won't hire you."

"Lookin' around, I figured as much," he mumbled, dropping back into his chair.

While the majority of the employees had abandoned their stations in favor of lunch, the few women on the floor and the lone colored man hauling parts out of the building offered him an idea of what constituted the population of the company.

"What do you have there?" She peered over his shoulder.

"Seein' what's out there."

She pointed to the listing under one ad already circled. "What about this one?"

"Can't see myself workin' as a seamstress."

"You're right. You won't even sew a loose button on a shirt."

"Ha, ha," he said as he circled an ad at the top of the page.

"You'll find something soon." Cass patted his shoulder before heading to the bedroom.

Randy hoped her prediction would come true. He wanted her away from the shipyard and back home with their children. And if the opportunity presented itself, he would not mind seeing her on the stage again, especially if he was standing by her side, accompanying her on the saxophone.

Cass emerged from the bedroom wearing a pink floral housedress, a pair of thick socks, and the bandanna. The outfit did nothing for her curves nor did it mask the stench of sweat that clung to her body.

Despite spending his early years around men who preferred to take food from a woman's child than to break a sweat, Randy had learned to respect the smell of hard work on a person at the end of the day. However, he still had trouble coming to terms with the odor coming from his wife.

"I'll have supper on the table shortly," she announced as she ducked into the bathroom.

Randy shuddered as the pipes banged and the water sputtered. Between the apartment and Cass's job, he felt like he had failed his family.

He had been conflicted when he received his draft notice. On one hand, he wanted to be a good citizen and do his part to help end the war and assure the soldiers returned home safely. However, at the time, he had a wife and one child, with another on the way. And though Cass was capable of taking care of the family, he should have been the one getting his hands dirty so they did not have to make do.

Randy stood and met Cass outside the kitchen.

"Here, take this." He reached into his pocket and pulled out his wallet. "Use what's in there to pay the rent and buy the groceries."

"What is that?"

"What I brought back with me."

"You hold onto that." She moved to step around him. "You may need to purchase a suit or something."

"I can't live off you." He stepped with her, blocking her retreat. "I won't." He lifted her hand and placed the billfold in her palm. "Take it. They're sendin' one last check to your parents' house. I should have somethin' by the time that money runs out."

Cass shook her head, but instead of arguing, she dropped the wallet into the pocket of her dress.

Randy placed his hands on her waist and pulled her to him. "I promise I'll get a job and things will get better." He lowered his head until their foreheads touched.

"You haven't been back a week." She wrapped her arms around his neck. Her fingers stroked his nape. "Don't worry; you'll find something soon."

He hoped she was right. Just as she did not sign up to be the sole breadwinner of the family, he did not sign up to be a kept man.

Chapter 6

Randy jerked his shoulder from the other man's touch. He did not want well wishes for future success or predictions of something coming his way soon. And he sure as hell did not want a reassuring pat on the shoulder from someone denying him the opportunity to provide for his family.

With a curt nod, he walked out of the warehouse, the fourth stop that morning—the umpteenth stop since his return two weeks earlier—in his search for a job. He was certain he had heard more excuses as to why he could not be hired than recruitment officers heard from young men who wanted to avoid the draft. His previous experience meant nothing; neither did his willingness to learn nor his eagerness to work.

Outside, Randy slipped his hand into his pants pocket and muttered a curse when his fingertips grazed lint. He had smoked the last cigarette from the carton he'd bought on the trip home. Having expected to find a job a lot sooner, he had given all his money to Cass, and his pride would not allow him to ask her for the dollar-fifty he needed to purchase another carton.

With a sigh, he glanced at the newspaper he'd hoped to ditch by the end of the day. He pulled a pencil from his coat pocket and, with the worn tip, drew a line through the ad he had circled that morning.

"Hey, I overheard you askin' for work."

Randy turned back to the group of men loitering near the entrance. A man whose hair was starting to grow out of its crewcut took a drag from his cigarette as he stepped forward.

"Shippin' office down the way is hirin'," the man continued. "Just ask for Kurt."

"Thanks." Randy eyed the cigarette pinched between the thumb and index finger of his informant's right hand. "Can I bum a cigarette?"

The man fished a half-empty pack from the front pocket of his shirt, and Randy pulled a battered cigarette from it.

"You need a light?"

Randy smoothed the cigarette, then accepted the lighter. The smoke slid down his chest and filled his lungs.

"When you get back?" the man asked, tucking the lighter in his pocket, next to the pack.

"About two weeks ago."

The man's head bobbed up and down. "Been back three weeks, myself." He took a drag from his cigarette. "Things haven't been easy. Was two weeks before I got this from a friend of a friend."

The news eased Randy's mind. At least he wasn't the only person having trouble finding work. There was still hope for him.

The man rambled off the name and exact location of the potential job before the foreman stuck his head out of the building and called his employees back in. Randy finished the bummed cigarette, then strolled down the dock.

It would feel good to get back to work; to contribute to the household and society. He could not fathom how some men were able to go weeks, months, or even years living off the charity offered to them.

After a fifteen-minute stroll, the building came into sight. Randy took a deep breath. He was ready to go for it. When he walked out, he would do so with his head held high with pride and a job to his name.

Randy opened the door and marched into the building. He stopped short and the door slammed into his back.

A handwritten note hung on the wall, announcing those who were not welcomed in the establishment. While there was no mention of saxophone-playing ex-soldiers, he could not, in good conscience, work in a place where a person was judged by his race, religion, or ethnicity.

"You need help?" A portly man asked, stepping between him and the sign.

Randy shook his head. "Wrong buildin'," he replied, pushing the lever on the door.

Ignoring the man's offer for directions, he stepped back outside. As the door clicked shut behind him, he glanced at the newspaper for the address to his next stop.

****

"Some help here," Cass called out while kicking the door. She fought to maintain her grip on the brown paper bag in her left arm while trying not to drop the eggs that threatened to spill from the bag in her right arm. The last thing she wanted to do was visit the market a second time when she still had chores to tend to.

She pulled her foot back and swung it forward with enough force to wake Randy in the event he was sleeping. However, instead of slamming into the wooden barrier, it continued forward until the size six men's work boot she wore collided with soft flesh.

"Son-of-a—" Randy's curse was drowned out by her expletive. He grabbed his calf and fell against the doorjamb.

Not expecting his help anytime soon, Cass slipped past him and dropped the bags on top of the newspapers covering the table.

"Sorry, hon," she said.

"That's okay." He pushed away from the wall and limped to the table. "Ain't like I needed this leg for walkin'."

Cass rolled her eyes as she walked over and closed the door. Could the man be any more melodramatic?

"How'd it go today?"

"What do you think?" He waved at the newspapers that were opened to the help wanted ads.

At least the unintentional assault was not the only reason he was going to be surly that evening.

"Damn, I think you cut the skin," he mumbled, pulling up his pants leg.

"Go in the bathroom and put some alcohol on it." She nudged his shoulder. "There's some in the medicine cabinet."

Muttering a string of curses under his breath, Randy limped toward the bathroom. Cass rolled her eyes. She was certain she hadn't kicked him that hard. Even so, there was no cause for him to go on like he was.

Cass draped her coat over the back of the chair and carried a bag to the kitchen. She had the taste for fried pork chops and okra but lacked the energy needed to prepare the meal. That morning, a repair had taken longer than anticipated, and she and Doreen had to work through lunch to finish the job on time. Later that afternoon, a cantankerous driver refused to unload supplies from a truck, forcing the women to lift crates that weighed more than fifty pounds.

Unfortunately, her arrival home did not signal the end of her day. After she put dinner on the stove, she would need to rinse the load of clothes that had been soaking in the bathtub all day. Then she would carry them downstairs and hang them on the line stretched between two poles erected behind the building.

"What's this?"

Cass pulled her head out of the icebox, where she had been trying to figure out what she was in the mood to cook. She peered over the door at the carton of cigarettes Randy held in the air.

"I noticed you ran out last night," she replied. In truth, she had purchased the groceries and was walking toward the door when a man stepped into the store and asked for a pack. His request reminded her of the crumpled wrapper she had seen in the trash when she was cleaning the kitchen the previous night.

She had thought the purchase would make him happy, but his frown said he was anything but.

"What's wrong?" she asked.

He opened his mouth, then shook his head. "Nothin'," he mumbled.

That one word contradicted the downturned corners of his lips and the lines surrounding his eyes.

Cass closed the icebox. "I don't have time for guessing games." She crossed her arms over her chest and leaned against the appliance. "What's bothering you?"

He hesitated a second before blurting out, "I don't want you buyin' me cigarettes."

"Why? You were out, so I picked some up. What's the big deal?"

"Don't do it again." He dropped the carton on the table and walked into the bedroom before she could ask him to elaborate.

She pushed away from the icebox and took one step before she stopped. While the temptation to follow him was great, she had neither the time nor the inclination to soothe hurt feelings.

Deciding to satisfy her cravings, she turned to the icebox and pulled out the pork chops she had placed inside minutes earlier.

****

The meal had to have been the toughest Randy had to swallow. It was not so much his inability to contribute to the household that had him picking at Cass's fried pork chops and okra, but the argument he nearly started because of it.

The cigarettes had been a thoughtful gesture, one he was certain she made without any intention of later throwing it back in his face that they were purchased with her money. Yet instead of showing his gratitude, he'd all but tossed the carton back at her.

The door opened and a breeze rushed in ahead of Cass. She shivered in the sweater she tossed over her shoulders whenever she planned to be outside for only a few minutes.

Randy pushed up from the table and walked over to her as she closed the door.

"Those clothes are goin' to freeze out there. Why

didn't you hang them in the bathroom?" He rubbed her arms to help her warm up.

"I didn't want them dripping on the floor. I'll bring them in to thaw before I leave for work." She stepped around him and carried the tin washtub to the bathroom.

Randy bristled at the mention of her job. He did not know what irked him more, his lack of work or where she worked.

Determined not to offer his opinion and ruin what was left of their evening, he closed his eyes and counted back from ten. It was not her fault she had to resort to manual labor to make ends meet. The South did not offer the same opportunities as the North. It was one of the reasons he'd moved on when he became of age. The other had been his search for a place in which everyone was accepted regardless of their ancestry.

When he felt he had control over his tongue, he opened his eyes and followed her to the bathroom. He leaned against the doorframe and waited as she washed her face. Her thick braid rested between shoulders that were strong enough to bear the burden of the family's care.

Cass straightened and reached behind her for the towel draped over the side of the bathtub.

"Here you go." Randy stepped forward and grabbed the terrycloth. She jerked back and wiped the water from her eyes with the back of her hands. "Sorry to startle you."

She squinted through the drops of water hanging from her eyelashes.

He did not blame her for being hesitant. He had not been the most gracious spouse that evening.

Randy held the towel out to her. Another second

passed before she accepted the offer.

"Thank you for the cigarettes," he said as she dried her face. "I do appreciate them."

"You're welcome." Her reply was muffled by the towel. "I hope you didn't think I bought them to show off."

"I know you wouldn't do that. It was just my pride rearing its ugly head." He moved one step to the right, giving her access to the towel rack. "How 'bout I make it up to you?" He leaned forward and pressed his lips to hers.

Cass did not respond to the amorous gesture with enthusiasm. Fearing she was still mad, Randy pulled back and searched her face.

Instead of anger, he noticed something far worse. Her eyelids drooped under the weight of exhaustion. His gaze dropped to the same shoulders he had been admiring a minute earlier. While they were strong enough to bear so many responsibilities, they too were beginning to sag under the pressure of fatigue.

It did not take a genius to realize she did not need a husband climbing on top of her, trying to coax an orgasm from her. She needed an understanding man who was willing to put his needs aside for a night.

"Go to bed." Randy leaned in and kissed her forehead. "I'll be there in a minute."

"You're not going to join me?" She asked through a yawn.

"After I make sure the house is locked up."

Without further persuading, she shuffled to their room. Less than a minute later, the bed creaked as she plopped down.

In the morning, Randy would double his efforts to

find work. They…more specifically, she…could not keep going as they were.

Chapter 7

Cass dropped her lunchbox on the table and rushed across the room to investigate the tap at the window behind the sofa. The few times visitors had tossed pebbles at the building to get Martha Lynn's attention, Mr. Johnston had let it be known that he did not appreciate any abuse to the structure.

She knelt on the cushions, pushed up the window, and stuck her head out in the dark. A young man, illuminated by a dim light bulb attached to the rear of the building, lowered his hand. The remaining pebbles rained on the ground around his shoes.

"Martha Lynn up there?" A wide grin decorated a face that probably did not need a razor more than once a month. "Tell her Petey wants to speak to her."

When the young men from nearby Little College and sailors on leave first stopped by, Martha Lynn would invite them up for drinks. But after Mr. Johnston threatened to evict them because of the noise the woman and her guests made late into the night, her sister-in-law would make plans to meet up with the men at other locations.

"Didn't Martha Lynn tell y'all her *husband* was coming home?" Whenever she spoke to one of her sister-in-law's admirers, she emphasized the word "husband" to stress that the woman was not available. It never sat right with her to know the married woman hung out with other men, even if Martha Lynn insisted everything she did was innocent. From Cass's experience with Randy, something as innocent as a dance could lead to much more.

The young man shrugged his shoulders. "Figured she might find a way to get away from her old man."

Cass's eyes narrowed. That old man was her brother, and though he was on the north side of thirty, he would have no problem beating the insolence out of this whippersnapper.

"You should be lookin' for your own wife instead of sniffin' around a married woman." She waved her hand. "Go on and get, before I send Mr. Johnston after your raggedy behind. And don't you come back."

"You ain't gotta worry about that." He sucked his teeth. "Don't wanna be botherin' no old heifer like you."

With a growl, she ducked back into the apartment and slammed the window closed. She climbed off the sofa, spun around, then stopped at the sight of Randy standing in the bathroom doorway.

He crossed his arms over his chest and raised an eyebrow. "What was that about?"

While Cass knew she had done nothing wrong, she felt as if he was waiting for her to confess all her sins. His reaction angered her more than the young man's cruel words.

"I've had a hard day, and I still have to make dinner," she replied, walking past him to the bedroom. "I'm not in the mood for your allegations."

"Seems like the kind of reaction one would expect from someone who was guilty of somethin'."

She faced him and cocked an eyebrow. "You care

to elaborate?"

"All I asked was, 'What was that about?' You're the one who got defensive."

"Maybe 'cause it's not what you said but how you said it." She snatched open the closet door and yanked her housedress off its hanger. "All the time you were away, I remained faithful to my wedding vows." She held up her left hand and wiggled the third finger that was adorned with a thin gold band and a diamond engagement ring. "Don't make me regret havin' said them in the first place." She shoved past him into the bathroom.

****

The door slammed with a rage Randy had never heard come from his wife before. He was overwhelmed with guilt at having been the one to anger her.

Yes, he was frustrated at the daily rejections by potential employers, but that was no reason for him to take his foul mood out on her or make accusations against her character.

During his time in the service, more than one soldier in his unit received a "Dear John" letter, informing the unlucky recipient that his wife had decided to go off with someone else. Then there were the few who sent updates that after they had been discharged their wives confessed they no longer had feelings for them.

No matter how many stories he heard, he had always remained confident that Cass was faithful and would be there for him. And when he returned, she had proved him correct.

Every day she came home from work and, upon learning that he still had not found a job, offered him words of encouragement. She did not accuse him of not trying hard enough or remind him that it was her paycheck getting them from day to day.

When Cass opened the bathroom door, she wore her pink housedress. Her dungarees and shirt were draped over the shower curtain rod, and her boots were in her hand.

A firm believer in spitting out his apologies instead of beating around the bush, Randy stepped in Cass's path and got straight to the point. "I'm sorry for the insinuation."

Because of what he had hinted at, he would not have blamed her if she barreled through him. However, demonstrating she was a bigger person than he was, she dropped the boots and embraced him.

"I'm sorry too. I know how that must've looked."

His arms wrapped around her, and he held her tight. He did not think there were too many women willing to stick by a man who continually stuck his foot in his mouth. He did not know what he had done to deserve a wife like her. What he did know, however, was that he needed to get it together soon. There was no telling how long she would be willing to put up with him.

"How 'bout I make it up to you?" He had been wanting to do something nice for her since receiving his last check from the service. He took her hand, led her to the table, and pulled a page from beneath the stack of newspapers. "We could take in a movie, then get a bite afterwards."

"What fun would that be with me sitting in the balcony and you in the orchestra? And let's not forget that we'll have to eat at separate restaurants."

"I'll sit in the balcony."

Cass tilted her head and placed her fists on her hips. She glared at him as if he had taken leave of his senses.

"Did you bump your head while you were in the service?"

"No, why?"

"'Cause you seem to be forgetting that we're not up North. We're in the South, where we can't just stroll into the theater together and expect all we'll have to worry about is a few dirty looks and snide remarks. They'd drag both of us out of there, and we'd be lucky if all they did was toss us in jail."

It wasn't like Randy was a stranger to the ways of the South. He knew there were laws that allowed owners to dictate who could frequent their establishments, which doors each group had to enter and where everyone had to sit. And only someone looking for trouble would challenge the rules.

"But I'm sick of hidin' in here each night. Ain't like there's anythin' to do other than stare at these four walls."

"My company's not good enough for you?"

"It would be if you stayed awake long enough for me to enjoy it."

On more than one occasion, she had fallen asleep in the middle of a conversation. And once or twice she had turned her back to him, after climbing in bed, and asked him not to touch her.

"How dare I be tired after working eight hours!" She jumped back as he reached for her. "You want to go out, then go." She waved him toward the door. "Just do me a favor and try not to wake me up when you return, 'cause *I* have work in the morning." She marched to the bedroom and slammed the door.

Taking her advice, Randy stormed out of the apartment, down the steps, and around to the front of the building. He stopped where there would have been a curb if they were farther into town. He glanced up and down the deserted road, which offered no suggestions for which direction he should take.

However, he did not need a sign to tell him he should go back upstairs, apologize, and then try not to say something stupid. While the first two tasks were not difficult, the last one seemed to be close to impossible. Lately, nothing sensible seemed to be coming out of his mouth.

Who was he to demand her attention at night when she was the one working all day? If anything, he should consider her refusal his punishment for allowing the burden of the family to fall on her shoulders.

"Waitin' on a bus?"

Randy turned to Mr. Johnston, who stood in the doorway of the store.

The man held out a bottle of soda. "Figured you might want one of these, considerin' you got a long wait ahead of you."

"Take it the bus don't stop here often." Randy walked toward the man and accepted the generous offer.

Mr. Johnston tilted his head to one side and thought for a second. "Last time the bus stopped here was…well, never."

Despite his sour mood, Randy smiled at the joke. "In that case, I better make this last." Using the bottle opener attached to the door frame, he popped off the cap. The small piece of metal fell to the floor with a clank.

"Leave it," Mr. Johnston said as Randy started to bend down to pick up the cap. "Grandkid collects them for skully."

Randy took a healthy swig of the cold, sweet beverage. It had been weeks since he'd enjoyed something other than milk or water.

"Wish I could offer you somethin' stronger," Mr. Johnston said, "but my wife, rest her soul, could never abide by anyone drinkin' in her house."

Cass had told Randy their landlord had been a widower for fifteen years. The man respecting the woman's wishes even after she was gone for so long showed how much he loved her.

"You need somethin' stronger, there's a juke joint down the road." Mr. Johnston stepped into the store. "Course, there ain't no tellin' if you'd be welcome there."

"This is fine." Randy followed the man into the building and sat on a crate next to a table with a checkerboard laid out.

"You and the missus havin' an argument?"

"You heard us?"

"Nah, I didn't hear y'all. Cass never makes a peep." The man perched on a crate on the other side of the table and moved a black wooden game piece one space. "Course, that door slammin' kinda tips off a person."

"Sorry 'bout that." Randy placed his bottle on the floor by his feet, then moved a red piece.

"Just remember, new doors don't come cheap."

Randy made a note of the not-so-subtle warning.

He did not want to owe the man more than the six dollars they paid him each week for the apartment.

"So, what y'all fightin' about?" Mr. Johnston asked over the hum of the ice chest next to the door.

"What aren't we fightin' about would be easier to answer." Randy snorted. "Thing's aren't how I expected them to be."

The man chuckled. While Randy did not see anything amusing in what he said, out of respect for the older man, he took another drink of his soda and kept his comment to himself.

"Expected you'd come back home to a job that'd been waitin' for you and a wife willin' to drop everythin' to be at your beck and call?"

Mr. Johnston had it partially right. Randy had expected to get a job and support his family the way men were supposed to do. However, he had not expected Cass to jump at his demands. She'd sooner tell him what he could kiss if he tried bossing her around.

"I was twenty-two and married with a kid when I was drafted for the Great War," the man reminisced. "I thought bein' away from my family was tough, but I learnt comin' back was even harder. My family came out to welcome me when I got back, but once they returned to their homes, no one gave a damn about me.

"My first night home, my son opened the door, said it had been nice that I stopped by but it was time for me to go. I think it took him a month before he got used to the idea that I was there for good. There was no job waitin' for me. My wife and I had to struggle to make ends meet. But that wasn't even the worst of it."

Randy figured the man had not gone to the trouble of telling the story if he didn't plan on finishing it.

Therefore, instead of asking what could be worse than everything he was going through, he absently moved his checker piece.

The move cost him a piece and allowed the other player to advance to the other side of the board. Mr. Johnston reached across the table, grabbed one of his captured pieces, and crowned himself.

"Back then, I'd been foolish enough to think my service would mean somethin' to everyone around here. But it meant nothin'. I walked down the street and people didn't see a man who'd served his country. All they saw was another colored man, not worthy of their respect."

While it was reassuring he was not the only one who found it difficult when he returned home, it was more important for Randy to know the answer to his next question: "What do you suggest I do?"

"Be patient," Mr. Johnston said, jumping his king over the remaining red pieces. "Everythin' will work out in time."

It was sound advice. The problem was, patience wasn't one of Randy's virtues.

Chapter 8

Randy was ready to throw in the towel.

He was tired of the arguments, tired of his family pushing him away, and tired of being patient. But most of all, he was tired of pretending everything was fine in front of his in-laws.

As the muscles in his face gave out, the smile he had plastered on his face before emerging from the bedroom to celebrate Christmas faded. He was not in a celebratory mood, and he would have skipped the festivities had it not meant so much to Cass that they were together as a family for the first time in two years.

Cass's laughter drifted across her parents' living room as she traded barbs with Joe Frank, who appeared to have adjusted to civilian life better than Randy. The man had no trouble jumping back into his old job as a porter for the railroad. And unlike Sylvia and Shara, who refused to come within three yards of Randy, Joe Frank's eldest daughter glued herself to her father's side whenever he was home.

Deciding he needed a moment to himself to regroup, Randy excused himself from the circle that included his father-in-law and the man's two eldest sons. He fished a pack of cigarettes out of his pants pocket as he headed toward the door.

A cool breeze caressed his brow, which had become clammy from sitting in an overcrowded room.

He welcomed the soft tap of his shoes against the steps over the multiple conversations that had grown progressively louder with the arrival of more relatives.

Randy lit his cigarette as he weaved around the cars parked in the yard until he made it to the barn. He inhaled as he leaned against the structure and watched the smoke dance in front of him.

The first time he had visited the farm was Christmas 1939. Though they had been married for five months, Randy was aware that Cass had yet to break the news to her family. Her elopement with her first husband had resulted in her being disowned for two years, and she was nervous about her parents' reaction to the news that she had now married a white man.

Hoping to reunite the family who had not seen each other in eight years and possibly earn some points, Randy decided to surprise her with the trip home. They had left their apartment in D.C. before daybreak with the pretense of driving to New York to visit friends. However, once she was settled in the car, Cass fell asleep, making it easy for him to point the car south to deliver her to her present.

During the drive, Randy worried about the family accepting him and whether Cass would choose to honor her vows or the fifth commandment if they disapproved of her marriage. Thankfully, she had not been put in the position of having to choose.

There had been no mistaking the shock on her parents' faces when she introduced Randy to everyone. However, after a minute, he was welcomed into the home.

That was not to say everything has been fine since that day. Though he never mentioned it, he saw the suspicion in his father-in-law's eyes, and he was aware that Cass's four oldest brothers were concerned for her. However, Mother Porter treated him as one of her own, and he made a friend with Joe Frank.

A second pair of soles tapped against the planks on the porch. Since their last argument, two weeks earlier, Cass had put up a wall that he had yet to pierce. While she remained civil to him in the presence of others, the tone of her voice and the tension in her posture indicated she was not willing to share any part of herself—neither her body nor her mind—with him. He was therefore certain the footsteps did not belong to the woman he'd married.

Randy prayed the escapee was someone taking a trip to the outhouse. His hopes, however, faded as the celebrant's footsteps grew louder. He could not catch a break. Even five minutes to himself was too much to ask of his maker.

Martha Lynn peered around the corner. Her face brightened as her gaze locked on Randy. With a sway in her hips, she sashayed toward him. Her easy movements reminded him of a cat stalking a tom. He half expected her to drop on all fours and present herself to him.

When he was introduced to Martha Lynn, the woman's gaze had slowly wandered from the top of his head to his feet, lingering at his groin for a second more than necessary. He was a bit taken aback by the attention but concluded that Martha Lynn, who had been eight months pregnant at the time, was simply a flirt and would not chase after her sister-in-law's husband, especially with her own husband standing right beside her.

"You've a spare?" She pointed to his cigarette.

Though Randy had never seen the woman with a cigarette before, he reached into his pocket and pulled out the pack. She took one, then waited for him to exchange the pack for his silver lighter.

The flame reached forward and ignited the tip. Martha Lynn took a short drag and waited a heartbeat before she puckered her lips and released the smoke.

"So what brings you out here?" she asked.

"I needed a moment to myself," he replied.

Instead of taking the hint, Martha Lynn leaned against the doorframe, pushing her generous chest forward. "What for?"

"Don't need to burden you with my problems," Randy replied, forcing his eyes to remain north of her neck.

"But I'm a good listener." When he did not immediately offer an answer, she asked, "Problems with Cassie Ann?"

He flinched at the accuracy of her guess. She smirked; her eyes danced with a know-it-all glint.

"Not too hard to read the signs when you know men like I do." Martha Lynn took another drag off her cigarette and shrugged. "Cassie Ann hasn't said a word to you all morning, and you've been sitting in the same spot, sulking."

Her comment reminded him of the visitor two weeks earlier. He wondered just how well she knew men, and more importantly, had Cass gained the same knowledge while he was away.

As quickly as the thought popped into his mind, Randy pushed it out. Though the saying went, "You can judge a person by the company she keeps," it was not true of Cass.

When he and Cass had first met, she was friends with a woman who would not mourn the end of a relationship for any longer than it took to clean the man's belongings out of her apartment. Cass, however, had been more cautious, and it was over four years after the end of her first marriage before she was willing to take a chance with anyone else.

"Everything'll work out once I get a job," he replied.

"Good luck with that. There's nothing down here."

She was a wealth of information, telling him something he already knew.

Her chatter reassured him that she did not know men as well as she thought. Had she the slightest clue about him, she would have walked away and left him to his thoughts. Instead of verbalizing the sarcastic comments racing through his head, he took a drag from his cigarette.

"Have you thought about going north?" she asked.

Every minute of every day, he thought. Just that morning, he had considered bringing up the subject, but then he considered the toll the move would take on his family. If Cass remained behind, she would have to take care of the children by herself until he was settled and in a position to send for them. And he could not uproot the family with no idea where they would lay their heads when they got there.

"It's not that easy," he said. "I've got Cass and the girls to think of."

"It's a shame for a talent like yours to go to waste down here."

Martha Lynn pushed away from the wall, reached

out, and stroked his arm. A current flowed from the limb to the one body part she—and no other woman but Cass, for that matter—had no business affecting.

He looked at the woman as if he had never looked at her before. She was fair enough to be considered "high yella" and had "good" hair that hung loose over her shoulders. Her ample bosom left little room in her blouse, while her shapely legs reached from under a skirt that was barely loose enough to be considered decent.

Guilt slammed into his gut like a wrecking ball. He had no right to look at other women. His wife's lack of interest in sex was his fault, and until he made things right he needed to rely on his hand to satisfy his needs.

Randy jerked his arm away from Martha Lynn. "I need to get back before Cass wonders where I wandered off to." He dropped his cigarette butt on the ground and crushed it underneath his heel.

He felt her gaze on his back as he marched toward the house. His sixth sense told him she was not going to give up that easily and he would need to watch himself around her.

****

The breeze that blew through the room alerted Cass to Randy's return. She glanced over her shoulder and watched as he closed the door before he dropped back into the seat he had abandoned minutes earlier.

She had to give it to him. He had worked hard to maintain a pleasant disposition throughout the day. His smile had never faltered, not even when Sylvia and Shara politely thanked him for their rag dolls with no more enthusiasm than one would give to a stranger who gave them gloves for Christmas. However, she had noticed the lack of spark in his eyes, the slouch in his posture, and the monotone voice he used when he offered curt, one- or two-word answers to all inquiries.

As if he felt her gaze on him, he glanced up. Their eyes locked, and she held her breath. It was just over a month since she'd been overjoyed by his return. He had sat in the same spot, next to her father, laughing at Joe Frank's anecdotes. Occasionally she would glance in his direction and he would leer at her, silently conveying the fun they would enjoy once they were alone.

Randy did not offer her a teasing glint or even the hint of a smile. She only saw guilt in his eyes before he turned away.

"I need you in the kitchen," her mother mumbled, tugging on Cass's sleeve as she walked by.

Dejected by her husband's response, she followed the woman to the other building.

"What do you need help with?" Cass asked, glancing around the room for any item they'd failed to prepare the night before.

The turkey and ham were warming on the back of the stove. Covered dishes were stacked on every surface and included a variety of sides, from dressing to greens to her favorite, her mother's cornbread. Desserts sat on the table in the other room, where the women could keep a close eye out for anyone who would try to sneak a sweet.

"I want you to take the girls with you when you return to Norfolk tonight," her mother replied, using a dishtowel to protect her hand from the heat as she removed the lid from the pot of mustard and collard greens.

Cass chuckled. "They finally wore you out," she teased, settling in the corner opposite the stove to ward off the cold air blowing in from the opened door.

"You know they've done no such a thing." Her mother placed the pot's lid on top of another pan, then lightly snapped the towel at her.

"Then why?" Her amusement faded.

"Those girls are not gonna get used to their daddy if he's not around."

"We were hoping to take them back once Randy found a job and I quit mine." She picked at the corner of the green-and-white-checkered towel draped over the pan of sweet potatoes on the shelf next to her arm.

"I know, but it could be another week or another month before he finds somethin'. In the meantime, the girls don't know their daddy." Her mother placed a hand over hers and offered her a reassuring squeeze. "Those girls act like he's some stranger you dragged home." She shook her head and frowned as if it had been the most tragic sight she'd ever witnessed. "Until he finds somethin', he could watch the girls and let 'em get used to him."

While her mother made sense, Cass was not sure how to approach Randy with the suggestion—or if she even wanted to bring it up. They'd had so many arguments over the past few weeks, she was hoping for one day of peace. To suggest he stay home with the girls while she supported the family could lead to their worst fight ever.

Her first husband would have balked at the suggestion and insisted that raising children was woman's work. At the same time, he did not do what was considered man's work and support his wife.

During their two years together, he'd offered one excuse after another as to why he had yet to find a job. Foremen didn't hire him because they were afraid he'd go after their jobs; the dudes were jealous of him; the job was beneath him. Yet, on a Saturday, he would meet her at the door expecting her to hand over her money so he could go out with the boys.

Considering how different both men were, maybe Randy would not make a scene when he rejected the suggestion, but calmly discuss alternatives. Not likely.

"If you'd like, I'll talk to Randy," her mother offered.

Not only did Cass like the idea, but she would have preferred if the woman waited until Cass was in another state. However, it was not her mother's place to smooth things over with Randy. Cass had to make the suggestion to her husband and deal with the fallout.

"I'll do it." She patted her mother's hand before she slipped out of the kitchen.

Though the building was attached to the house and it was less than four yards from door to door, a knot formed in her stomach in the time it took her to walk that distance. She was not concerned Randy would go off in a rage. Such extreme behavior was reserved for those who threatened his family and property. However, she did not know how much more of his brooding she'd be able to take.

Cass stepped into the house and waited until Randy glanced in her direction again. She jerked her head toward the door before backing out and into Martha Lynn.

"What you up to, Cassie Ann?"

The woman's snide tone grated on Cass's nerves.

Growing up, whenever Martha Lynn and she were in the same room, it would not take more than a minute before her future sister-in-law was rubbing her advantages in Cass's face.

As the daughter of a storekeeper, Martha Lynn enjoyed the privileges that came from having money. Her dresses were store-bought, she had so many toys she couldn't keep track of all of them, and she never had to wake before sun-up to work in the fields.

Cass's mother used to say such indulgence would only breed a spoiled, out-of-control young woman. Despite the prediction, when they were younger, Cass would have traded families with the girl in a heartbeat.

"I could ask the same about you, Martha Lynn," Cass replied.

"Thought I'd come out here and catch a smoke."

Cass thought it was interesting, the woman's sudden desire to smoke when Randy stepped outside. She, however, pushed aside the accusatory thoughts. Though Martha Lynn could be a bit outgoing, she would give the woman the benefit of the doubt. Surely her sister-in-law would not make any inappropriate moves toward another woman's husband, especially with the woman close by. She also wanted to believe Martha Lynn would not do anything to shame Joe Frank, who had stood by her when she was in trouble.

"I came out here to talk to my husband," Cass announced.

"You mean emasculate him more than you already have." Martha Lynn's upper lip curled back in disgust.

"What are you talking about?"

"I heard you and your mother plotting against Randy," the woman clarified. "To ask a man to watch the children while you go out and work? Why don't you just ask him to hand over his balls while you're at it?"

"I should be honored to look after my children."

Cass glanced back at Randy, who stood less than a foot behind her. His scowl said he not only had heard the conversation but did not appreciate the other woman's comments.

Before Martha Lynn could argue with him, Cass threw out, "Don't you think you should go inside and give Joe Frank a break from looking after *your* children?"

Randy stepped aside and waved toward the room, where Joe Frank had spent the morning playing with the children while Martha Lynn posed in an armchair and showed off her new dress and shoes.

With her lips pursed, Martha Lynn brushed past Randy. He showed no reaction to the unnecessary contact. However, for the first time since they were in school, Cass felt inadequate around her sister-in-law.

Despite the years she had sung in clubs in New York and Washington, D.C., her clothes were still homemade. Her hair was plaited into one braid instead of styled and allowed to hang free over her shoulders. And though they were filed into neat ovals, her nails were short and her hands were rough from the chores she had been required to perform since her fifth birthday.

"I'm sorry you had to hear that," she said.

With his hand on the small of her back, Randy led her down the steps and away from the house. They stopped next to the hickory tree, and Cass's cheeks warmed as memories of his first night back resurfaced.

After coming together in the kitchen, they had

proceeded to the bedroom, where they spent the next couple of hours getting reacquainted with each other's bodies. They had taken their time remembering what turned them on, until they came so hard they did not have the energy to untangle their limbs afterwards.

She wanted to relive that night, feel his touch, and hear him call her name before he brought them both over the edge. But though her body was willing, all her mind wanted to do was sleep after she got in from work.

He leaned against the tree trunk and pulled her to him. His arms snaked around her waist, and hers rested on his shoulders.

"You really think I should watch the girls while you work?" he asked.

"Momma thinks this is a good opportunity for the girls to get to know you."

"And what about you?" He leaned forward until his forehead rested against hers. "What do you want?"

That question was too easy. She wanted world peace and a promise that her husband would never be taken away from her again. She wanted to live in a world where their relationship was accepted. And she wanted to raise her girls in a society that would accept them for who they were on the inside and not judge them by what they looked like on the outside.

Knowing most of what she wanted would not be realized in her lifetime, she opted for the one wish they could work on together.

"I want us to be a family."

Chapter 9

The whirlwind that was Randy's wife flew out the door without so much as a goodbye. To be fair, she had pecked the girls on the cheeks before she grabbed her lunchbox and blew a kiss in his general direction.

Her typical morning routine would not have been so bothersome had she stopped to offer some directions on what to do with the two girls who stood in their underwear, clinging to their rag dolls, staring at him as if he were some creature from outer space. Though he was not a stranger to being around children, a parent or caregiver was usually close by to jump in when he finished entertaining them.

As Randy scratched the strands sticking up from his head, Mr. Johnston's grandson called out, "Wait up," as he raced down the road to catch up with his classmates.

He mentally berated himself at the obvious answer for what to do next. By the time he had arrived at the table, Cass had the girls cleaned and breakfast had been placed in front of them. But since children were not born knowing how to stay clean, traces of their meal covered their face and hands.

"Come on," he said as he turned to the bathroom.

To his relief, the girls followed him. While they were not ready to embrace him, they would at least be obedient. It was a start.

As Randy tried to figure out what he should do after they were clean and dressed, he turned on the faucet. Having gotten used to the knocking pipes, he failed to warn the girls. They jumped at the noise.

Randy could have slapped himself for the oversight. "It'll stop in a minute," he reassured them.

After the second clang, he adjusted the temperature. Sylvia peered over the sink that was too tall for her sister. To solve the problem, Randy ducked into the bedroom and retrieved the small stepstool Cass used to reach the shelf in the closet.

Randy placed Shara on the stool, then took the rag doll and tucked it under his arm. Sylvia watched as he wet a washcloth and cleaned her sister's face and hands.

He ended by tweaking the girl's nose. A warm surge coursed from his heart throughout his body at her soft giggle.

"One down, one to go." He placed Shara back on the floor and handed her the doll.

Once he'd rinsed out the washcloth, he bent down and cleaned Sylvia. Despite a tweak to her nose, she did not make a sound. She was more cautious than her sister; it would be harder to break through her defenses.

After the girls were clean, Randy herded them back to the living room. The suitcase filled with the girls' clothes sat in front of the sofa. By the time they had returned to the apartment the previous evening, Cass had been too tired to make the bed in Martha Lynn's old room. Instead, she'd spread a bed sheet over the sofa and had the girls sleep there.

The linen that had been used for the makeshift bed had been folded and draped over the back of the sofa. Randy placed the suitcase on the cushion, opened the lid, and stared at the selection of dresses he had to choose from.

Knowing Cass made the girls' clothes, he could only wonder when she found the time. Between working at the shipyard, keeping up the apartment, and traveling between Norfolk and Piney Woods, he was sure she had enough to do without adding sewing to her lists of chores.

Unable to decide which dresses the girls should wear, he waved to the suitcase. "Which one's your favorite?"

Sylvia hesitated before pointing to the white trim peeping from under the stack. He lifted a handful of clothes with one hand and held up the blue dress the trim was attached to.

"This one?"

The girl nodded.

He dropped the dresses onto the sofa, then dug through the remaining clothes until he found her sister's matching dress.

Despite the girls' squirming, he slipped the dresses on them and helped them into their socks and shoes. Once every button was closed and buckle fastened, he stood back and stared at the next hurdle…the curly tresses that had unraveled from their braids during the night.

Having never braided hair, he was unsure how to proceed and decided it was one task he would put off until Cass returned home that evening.

"What's next?" he mumbled, looking at the clothes flung across the furniture. He grabbed the dress closest to him and shoved it into the suitcase. As he reached for the second dress, he realized he could do better.

Randy gathered an armful of clothes and marched to Martha Lynn's bedroom. He pushed open the door and recoiled at the musky odor that smacked him in the face. Remnants of the woman's makeup, creams, and lotions covered the top of the dresser. A lone pink sponge curler lay in the middle of the floor. And he did not want to consider what bodily fluids had stained the sheets covering the bed.

His skin itched from looking at the mess. Cass, who liked a clean house, had most likely never stepped foot in the room before her sister-in-law moved out. However, had she known the state of it, she would have disinfected it the first night she had been able to enter.

There was no way his children would sleep in that room, at least not until he scrubbed every inch of the space.

Randy tossed the clothes back onto the sofa as he headed to the bathroom. The girls stood to the side and watched as he filled the pail with soap and water and gathered the mop and rags. They then followed him back to the room and stood in the doorway as he got rid of every trace of its previous resident.

Four hours later, Randy stood in the center of the room he had scrubbed from top to bottom with the lye soap. It would take several more hours before the mattress was dry enough for him to cover it with the clean sheets he'd located in the top of the closet in the other bedroom. He had, however, been able to hang up the girls' dresses and fill the drawers with their underwear and pajamas. Their toys sat under the window in a crate he got from Mr. Johnston.

"Daddy?"

Randy froze at the term of endearment uttered by

his eldest daughter. The last time she had addressed him by that term, she had wrapped her small arms around his neck and sent him off to the service with a little drool running down his cheek from the kiss she had given him.

His eyes filled with tears. While he was certain his mother-in-law had the right idea, he had not expected the girls to warm up to him so quickly.

"Daddy..." The voice was more persistent.

"Yes, darling." He turned to the girl. "What do you need?"

"Shara had an accident."

She pointed to her sister, who stood in the middle of a puddle forming on his clean floor.

****

Cass raced up the steps to the apartment, fearing what she would find inside. Guilt for her abrupt departure had weighed on her all day. She had meant to offer Randy a few tips before she left for work. However, getting the girls up, cleaned, and fed had taken her longer than she had anticipated, and she could not be late for work that morning.

"Mommy!" Sylvia and Shara squealed as Cass burst through the door, huffing from her haste to get home. They slid from their chairs at the table and threw themselves at her legs.

Randy walked from the sink with a dishrag in his hand and wiped up the milk that had sloshed over the side of Shara's cup in her haste to get to her mother before her sister.

Cass squatted down in front of the girls, kissed their foreheads, and marveled at the clean cherubs wearing towels around their necks.

"Inspectin' them to make sure they're in one piece?"

She knew he was joking and did not want to hurt his feelings by admitting she had been worried about his ability to handle the girls. Randy had always gotten along with the children in the neighborhoods they lived in, as well as her nieces and nephews. However, as far as she knew, he had never been alone with any for more than five minutes.

Cass had also worried about the girls' reaction to him. Though they no longer ducked behind other adults when he walked into a room, a part of her feared they would spend the day crying.

"What happened to their hair?" she asked, fingering the lock of hair that stuck straight out from Shara's head.

Randy offered her a sheepish grin. "I don't know how to braid."

"It's not that hard."

"Says the woman who probably learned on her doll twenty years ago."

Cass untangled herself from the arms clinging to her and stood. "I'll show you after I fix dinner."

"No need." He pointed to the pot on the stove.

The aroma of stewed chicken lured her into the apartment. She noticed the tray of biscuits next to an opened can.

"You cooked dinner?" she asked, reaching behind her to push the door closed.

"Sylvia and Shara had to eat."

True. However, she had expected him to offer them some bread with apple butter. The meal went beyond her expectations.

"I'll wash up, and then I'll show you how to do their hair, before I make their bed."

"Already done." Randy swung Shara back into her chair. The girl's squeal nearly drowned out, "I cleaned the room and burned Martha Lynn's sheets."

"Daddy scrubbed the floor two times," Sylvia added as she scrambled back into her chair.

"It was that bad?" Cass shuddered. Yes, her sister-in-law had never lifted a finger to help out around the house, but to be that filthy?

"Actually, Shara had an accident after I'd cleaned it the first time," Randy commented.

Cass's head dropped forward. "She's still training. You should take her to the bathroom every two hours." She could not believe she'd forgotten to mention that important detail.

"I kinda figured that much out myself." Randy walked over and picked up the lunchbox she'd placed on the floor in order to hug the girls. "Of course, we'll go over everythin' tonight so we don't have any surprises tomorrow."

"We can do that after we do their hair," she confirmed, walking to the bedroom.

Cass shrugged out of her coat and felt as if a weight heavier than the world had been lifted from her shoulders. With the chores completed, it was the first time she did not have to worry about taking care of someone else or the apartment after returning from work.

As she reached for the closet, she caught a glimpse of herself in the mirror hanging on the door. Normally, she did not give a fig about what she looked like. But for once she had more than a second to herself and decided she would take full advantage of it.

Cass hung up her coat, then dug in the back of her closet until she located the blue robe Randy had sent her from California on their first Christmas apart. She snatched the robe and the matching gown from the hanger and dashed out of the room.

"I'll be out in a few," she called over her shoulder as she ducked into the bathroom.

The hot shower was just the remedy for her tired, sore muscles. She had two more days until the weekend. And though she always looked forward to the time off, it would be extra special since she did not have to take a two-hour drive to see her children.

Using the loofah that came in a gift set Cass had treated herself to, she scrubbed her skin until it tingled. Afterwards, she rubbed lotion over her body, then slipped on the satin gown and robe. She pulled the bandanna off her head and frowned at the braid wrapped around her head. She wished she had time for something fancier, but she had promised to show Randy how to braid, which if not done would result in tangles that would be hell, for both her and the girls, to get out.

Cass tossed her dirty clothes into her room before stepping into the kitchen.

"Mommy's pretty," Sylvia announced.

"Pretty," Shara parroted.

Cass smiled, then waited for Randy to make a comment. As each second passed without a peep from him, her confidence failed. Maybe her appearance needed more work than she could manage in fifteen minutes.

After a heartbeat of silence, Cass felt silly for trying. She spun around to return to the bedroom and change into something more sensible, but the sight of Randy standing by the stove, staring at her, halted her retreat. His mouth hung open, and stew dripped from the serving spoon onto the floor.

"Randy, you're making a mess."

He jerked out of his trance and glanced down at the bits of chicken and carrots on the blue braided rug. With a flick of the wrist, he dropped the remaining stew on the plate, then tossed the spoon into the pot.

"Sorry. You caught me by surprise."

"Is that a good thing or bad?"

His gaze slowly moved down her body and, taking just as much time, up again. "It's good." He nodded. "Definitely good."

Cass's face warmed. Though he had married her despite her preference for canvas shoes over heels, she still worried about how she compared to other women, like Martha Lynn, who spent hours in front of the mirror fussing over their hair and makeup. It felt good to have him admire her after six years of marriage, two children, and her less than fashionable attire.

Cass joined Randy at the stove and finished preparing her plate as he wiped up the mess.

"What's with the new look?"

"I don't know." She shrugged her shoulders. "I was suddenly in the mood to clean up."

"How tired are you tonight?" She detected the hint of hope in his tone.

"I'm feeling fine." The shower had refreshed her, and she was certain the meal would provide the energy she needed to make it past the initial kiss and caress.

Randy traced the neckline of the housecoat. "Hold onto that feelin'." He pressed his lips to her forehead before tossing the dishrag into the sink and stepping out of the room.

By the time he returned, Cass had polished off her food and was stacking the dishes on top of each other.

"I'll take care of this," he offered, taking the dishes from her. "You get what you'll need for their hair."

Taking each girl by the wrist, Cass led them to the bathroom, where she removed the towels protecting their pajamas. After washing their hands and faces, she sent them to their bedroom to get their rag dolls and the book of nursery rhymes she had given them for Christmas.

When everyone finally met in the living room, Cass and Randy sat on the sofa, each with a girl between their legs.

"The main thing you have to remember," she said, passing him a comb, "is that patience will be your best friend."

Utilizing the virtue, Cass took her time showing him how to detangle his daughters' hair, moisturize it, and then twist it into two plaits. His first attempt resulted in braids she would allow her children to wear only to bed, but the process had been painless for all of them…with no tears from the girls or frazzled nerves for the parents. When the hair-care lesson was over, Cass read to the girls, then tucked them into bed.

"So how was your first day with the girls?" Cass asked as they stepped out of the bedroom.

"We survived."

"You sound surprised."

"I was nervous. What if somethin' happened to them? Or what if they started screamin' when you walked out, and refused to stop?"

Though he vocalized the same concerns that had been on her mind all day, she reassured him, "You would've figured something out."

"I probably would've sat down on the floor and joined them."

"I'm glad you didn't have to resort to such drastic measures." Cass draped her arms around his neck. "Also, thank you for everything you did today…cleaning the room, making the meals…"

Randy dipped his head and brought his lips close to hers. Most evenings, she turned from him, unwilling to encourage something she knew she would not be able to finish. However, her renewed energy had inspired her not only to clean up but to follow through on her gown's unspoken suggestion.

Cass closed the space between them. The sparks that had been missing in their life ignited. Her limbs shook. She wanted—no, she needed—to be with him.

Randy backed her up until she was against the wall, pushed his hips forward, and allowed her to feel his excitement. His condition was a boost to her ego. After weeks of her pushing him away, he still wanted her.

Cass's hand dropped to the front of Randy's pants and yanked on his belt. She felt a cool breeze on her legs as the hem of her gown inched up. They were eager to be together, to reaffirm their desire for one another.

"Mommy," Sylvia called.

Cass groaned at the interruption. It felt so good to have Randy pressing against her, she was tempted to ignore the child. Who knew when they would get another opportunity to be together?

"Mommy?"

The plea was louder, as if the girl was standing...

Randy pulled back and released Cass's gown. The material dropped back in place, covering her shaky limbs.

Cass knew she would admire her daughter's persistence later in life, but at that moment she would have settled for a child who gave up after the first try.

"What do you want?" Randy's tone was strained from his attempt to remain calm despite the undesired interruption.

"Mommy didn't kiss our dolls goodnight."

"Go back to bed. She'll be there in a minute."

"I'll be what?" Cass's voice rose an octave.

Two small sets of feet pattered back into the girls' bedroom. The springs creaked as they scrambled onto the bed.

Randy's head fell forward; his body shook with laughter.

"That's not funny," she fussed, pushing against his shoulder. "I go in there, and I'm liable to toss those dolls out the window."

"You can't do that." He gave her a chaste kiss on the cheek. "They'll only be young once."

Cass humphed.

"Besides, we can always continue where we left off...in sixteen years."

Chapter 10

"I'm bored." Martha Lynn dragged out her last word for two beats.

Cass could have ignored the woman's whining if the complaint had not been repeated every fifteen minutes for the past two hours. Even Sylvia and Shara had been less annoying during the two-hour ride from Piney Woods to Norfolk.

"When Joe Frank suggested we drive down here, I thought we'd head over to Church Street, not sit around your apartment." Martha Lynn held up her bottle of cola and frowned. "You're not even serving beer."

"You know Mr. Johnston doesn't like drinking in the apartment."

"That old buzzard don't know how to have fun." She peered around the room, her gaze stopping on Randy, who sat on the sofa next to Joe Frank. "Don't know why y'all haven't got something better."

"First of all, you need to treat Mr. Johnston with more respect." Cass waved the serving spoon at the man sitting on the chair she had set in front of the sofa. "Second of all, I don't see why I'd move away from here. The rent's good."

"That's the problem with your family. Always content with staying put. Never trying to move up in this world."

"If that's the case, why'd you hook up with Joe?"

"I ask myself that every day."

Cass was speechless. Yes, Joe Frank was not chasing after fame and fortune, but between his salary and the tips he collected, he brought in enough money for her sister-in-law to continue to enjoy the comforts she had when she was a child.

Martha Lynn did not have to rise before the sun to tend to the animals on a farm, then cook breakfast for the family before heading into the fields to help with the crops. And she did not have to steal a second here and there to sew the clothes on her back. Every morsel she set on her table was purchased from the grocery in town, as well as every stitch of clothing she wore.

Cass opened her mouth to remind the woman she could have done worse and married a man who lounged around all day while she struggled. The lecture was cut short before she started when Randy walked over and picked a piece of bacon from the pot of Hoppin' John on the stove.

"How's it goin' over here?" He popped the swiped food into his mouth.

"Boring," Martha Lynn replied before sashaying toward the sofa. Her hips moved as if she were trying to attract the attention of a roomful of men.

Randy did not spare the other woman a second glance. His gaze focused on Cass, his eyes twinkled with mischief, and his lips turned up into a smirk.

"What's so amusing?" she mumbled, turning back to the plate she had been preparing for their landlord.

He traced a line across her forehead. "You get this crease whenever Martha Lynn's around."

"You came over here to tell me that?"

"No, I came over here to keep you from clocking

her upside her head." He pulled the spoon from Cass's grip and dropped it into the bowl of potato salad he'd helped her prepare earlier. "So what has Martha Lynn said to upset you this time?"

Besides insulting her family, a transgression Cass would address another time? "She's been complaining ever since she walked in." She sighed. Though the woman's annoying disposition had been tap dancing on Cass's last nerve, her complaints dredged up memories of Randy's previous argument about their inability to go out on the town. Staying in and trading service stories with the men while the children ran around outside was not the rip-roaring evening they were used to.

"I couldn't ask for a better way to spend a Friday night." He tilted his head toward the bedroom. "Actually, I could..." He turned back to her and wiggled his eyebrows.

"What about the movies...going out to eat..."

"Guess bein' in isn't that bad when you have someone with you."

Cass usually shied away from public displays of affection, but she could not pass up the opportunity to show Randy how much she appreciated his comment.

Though everything was not back to the way it had been, they were no longer waking up in the morning frustrated from unspent desire. Once the girls were in bed, they had not only the time but the energy to demonstrate just how much they meant to each other.

"Hey, Cass!" Joe Frank called from across the room. "You know there's a soldier on your lips."

Randy pulled back and laughed.

"Don't encourage him," she scolded her husband

before glaring at her sibling. "Didn't Momma teach you not to overstay your welcome?"

"But we just got here a couple of hours ago." He draped his arm over the back of the sofa. Martha Lynn slid forward, away from her husband's touch. "Figure we have another two, three days before we get on your nerves," he joked, despite his wife's rejection.

"Try two to three minutes," Cass said over the knock at the door.

Martha Lynn's face lit up as she gaped at the door. Cass shook her head at the three men who turned to her and cocked their eyebrows. She knew as much as they did about the visitor. Her sister-in-law had been the outgoing one, who enjoyed entertaining around the clock, while Cass preferred peace and quiet in her home.

Cass opened the door and smiled. "What are you doing here?" She waved Doreen into the apartment.

"I needed to ask a favor." The woman crossed the threshold and glanced around the room. "I didn't mean to interrupt your party."

"It's just family."

Doreen stared at Martha Lynn. The other woman rolled her eyes and slumped back on the sofa. She instantly shot up when the sleeve of Joe Frank's shirt brushed her neck.

"If you don't mind." Doreen pointed outside. "It'll only take a minute."

Cass stepped out of the apartment and closed the door. The dim glow from the light attached to the side of the building illuminated a distance of three yards. The brisk air brushed her bare arms, reminding her that despite the mild afternoons the temperature tended to dip in the evenings.

"What's wrong?"

"You used to sing in a club," Doreen said.

"Yes, what about it?"

"I know this is last minute, but we didn't know till an hour ago, so I won't blame you if you say no—"

"I didn't realize it was so chilly out here." Cass hugged herself, hoping the woman would take the hint and speed things along.

"I'm sorry." Doreen pointed over the rail. "This is my brother, Zed."

The man stepped from the shadows into the light. "It's nice meetin' you, Miss Cass." He touched the brim of his hat. "Dory's told me a lot about you."

She tilted her head to him. "Nice meeting you." She managed to remain pleasant despite her impatience to get to the reason for their visit.

"Zed owns a juke joint up yonder," Doreen continued.

"The name's Zed's Palace," he added, his voice full of pride.

"Stop interrupting and let me talk."

"But you didn't tell 'er the name."

"I was getting to that."

Cass cleared her throat. She was afraid she would freeze by the time the siblings got to the point.

"Oh, yeah," Doreen mumbled as if she'd forgotten Cass was standing next to her. "Zed's singer had a fight with her old man and…well…she won't be able to perform for a while. It don't matter most nights, 'cause he has a band, but he wanted to have something special New Year's Eve."

"I'm flattered you thought about me," Cass

admitted. "But I don't work alone."

"Dory said you worked with your husband, but he's still in the service," Zed called up.

The weight of her lie by omission bore down on her. More than once she'd wanted to tell the women she was closest to at the shipyard about Randy's return, but what if they insisted on stopping by to meet him? Could they keep the relationship to themselves, or would the news spread through the shipyard faster than aphids in a vegetable garden? And if the news got out, would her job be in jeopardy?

"He's paying five dollars—" Doreen offered.

"Five dollars?"

"I...I meant seven?" The woman peered down at her brother who vigorously nodded his head. "Yes, that's right...seven."

Cass mentally praised herself for not laughing in the woman's face. The last time she stepped on stage, she was earning three times that amount each night.

"I need to think about this. How 'bout I stop by and let you know tomorrow?"

The worry lines on Doreen's face did not change.

"First thing in the morning," Cass added.

Doreen glanced down at her brother once more.

Around the corner, Avery counted to ten as her sister, cousins, and Mr. Johnston's grandson scrambled to find hiding places. The girl reached eight before Zed slowly nodded his head. He rattled off the directions and, despite her having yet to agree, promised the band would be present to rehearse when she arrived.

Cass muttered, "Good-bye," as she ducked back into the apartment.

"I was about to come after you," Randy said,

draping a sweater over her shoulders. "Thought she'd only be a minute."

Cass slipped her arms into the sleeves and hugged the thick wool close to her. "It took her that long to start hemming and hawing."

"What did li'l Dory want?" Martha Lynn asked.

Her dislike for her former co-workers equaled their dislike for her. At times this had led to disagreements, with both sides looking to Cass for support. Refusing to show solidarity with either, she would plead the fifth, then walk off to see where else she could be of use until the bickering stopped for the day.

"She wants me to sing at her brother's juke joint on New Year's Eve," she replied.

"What'd you say?" Randy asked over the murmurs in the room.

"I had to think about it."

"What's there to think about?"

"Randy, they think you're still in the service. I'd have to do this without you."

****

Before they came together as a couple, Cass and Randy had been partners on stage. When he played his saxophone, he played for her, and when she sang, she sang to him. He could not imagine performing without her and had turned down gigs because they only wanted him. However, he could not allow her to give up an opportunity to do what she loved…what she was born to do.

"How much are they payin'?"

"Seven dollars."

"An hour?"

"For the night."

He stared down at her, waiting for her to crack a smile. When her lips did not twitch he stated, "People used to pay you that just to walk through the door."

"I told you the places down here didn't pay much."

Even so, she had to accept the gig. He had never been one to turn down a job because the compensation did not meet his standards. He preferred to look at each opportunity as a means to move forward. They never knew who could be in the audience and what that person might have to offer.

"I want you to take the gig," he said.

"But what about you?"

"I get to sit in the audience and think about what I'll do when I get you home."

"You forget I'm here?" Joe Frank called from the sofa.

"No, but trust me, it wasn't for a lack of tryin'."

Cass's head fell forward; her body shook with the laughter she did not try to suppress. It was a sound he'd enjoyed before the war, and it had recently returned to their lives.

Though the girls had only been with them for three days, it was already feeling like the family he had been hoping to come home to. Each morning, he woke to a wife and two daughters, and they all ate breakfast together before sending his wife off to work. In the evenings, they ate dinner together, then read to the girls before tucking them into bed.

Yes, the arrangement was not conventional, and Randy held out hope that one day the roles would be reversed, with Cass staying at home with the girls while he supported the family. Or better yet, with them on stage together again. However, he was home, they were not arguing, and after the children were in bed, Cass was more receptive to spending time with him.

"You can't let this opportunity slip by." Randy brushed his fingertips across her jaw. "You'll be back on stage, where you belong."

Chapter 11

A fancy name did not enhance the ambiance of an establishment. Neither did the multi-colored confetti tossed over the tables and bar.

When Cass visited Zed's Palace on Saturday, the proprietor pointed to the litter on the floor and the lack of décor and insisted the place would be spruced up by New Year's Eve. Yet, two days later, it did not look like anything had been done beyond sweeping up the garbage and tossing tiny pieces of paper over the furniture.

In all fairness, Cass had seen juke joints more rundown than Zed's Palace. The establishment she'd visited with Martha Lynn a few months back to celebrate the woman's birthday had been a couple of tables set up in a back yard. The proprietor served watered-down booze and overcooked chicken, while the musicians played the same three songs over and over again throughout the evening.

At least the shed that was home to Zed's Palace had four walls, a roof, and ample space in the center of the room where the patrons could show off their moves after consuming the mouthwatering ribs and catfish that was cooked out back.

"What do you think?" Doreen tossed a handful of confetti at the short platform that had been erected near the door for the band. The drummer and pianist muttered curses as they waved the small pieces of paper off their instruments.

Not wanting to squash the woman's enthusiasm, Cass merely nodded her head and smiled.

The woman squealed and clapped her hands like a child excited for the praise she received, then toddled away on heels too high for her.

"Girl's going to break her neck trying to play grownup in those shoes," Martha Lynn said, making no attempt to lower her voice.

"Leave her be," Cass said. "She looks nice." She mentally patted herself on the back for uttering the lie with a straight face. In reality, her co-worker looked like a young girl playing dress-up in her mother's clothes. Her red dress hung over a frame that could have belonged to a prepubescent child, and besides being too high, her matching shoes were a size too big on her.

"Ain't saying a word. Looking forward to seeing her fall on her behind."

Cass rolled her eyes. "Twelve more hours." She mumbled the countdown she'd started that morning. Though she enjoyed having her brother around and she would miss Avery and June, she could not wait until the family—or more specifically, Martha Lynn—departed for Piney Woods.

All weekend, Martha Lynn had behaved as if they were attending a gala with President Truman and King George VI. The woman would not lift a finger to help out around the apartment, lest she muss her hair, which she'd had styled at the beauty salon on Saturday, or chip her nails, which had been polished on Sunday. Instead, she spent her time fussing over her wardrobe, finally selecting a red, off-the-shoulder, ankle-length dress that would make it impossible for her to do anything other than prance around and show off.

Martha Lynn's refusal to help did not grate on Cass's nerves as much as the woman's criticism about everyone around her. Just as she had done when they were children, her sister-in-law put others down for what they lacked in their closets.

Determined not to let Martha Lynn annoy her, Cass strolled to the far end of the room, to the bar that stocked a variety of liquors that guaranteed that those who imbibed did not feel anything after a few shots. She stopped along the way to chat with women she knew from the shipyard and a few she bumped into each week at the grocery.

"Surprised to see this place packed," Bertha commented when Cass reached her destination fifteen minutes after she'd started toward the bar.

"Doreen said they usually get a good crowd."

"And you haven't figured out by now that girl has a tendency to stretch the truth? This place ain't never seen business like this."

Cass nodded to the bartender, who placed a beer in front of her. Before she had been able to get a word out on Saturday, Zed sweetened his offer by adding free drinks to the deal. Instead of revealing that she'd already made up her mind, she took a minute to "think" about the offer.

When she had finally agreed to do the gig, the brother and sister insisted she drove a hard bargain before patting themselves on the back for a job well done.

"If it's not usually this crowded, what got everyone

down here?" Cass asked.

"As soon as you agreed to sing, they started spreadin' the word that they finally got a real singer. After the rehearsals, the band backed them up." Bertha dropped two quarters on the bar. Once the bartender removed the money and placed a beer in its place, she turned back to Cass. "So what sin did you commit to get stuck with her?" She pointed her bottle at Martha Lynn.

The woman had arrived early with Cass to commandeer a table near the stage for Randy, Joe Frank, and her. However, instead of guarding the seats, she had strolled onto the stage to talk to the drummer.

"She and my brother came down with the children for the weekend. After I agreed to sing here, they decided to stay a few more days to see the show."

"Well, where's that brother of yours?" Bertha glanced around the room.

"His daughter is watching the other children. He wanted to make sure she had everything before he headed on over here."

"Look forward to meetin' him. The only person you talked about more was your husband. When will he be down here?"

"Soon." Cass took a sip of her beer. Though she knew the woman was inquiring as to when Randy would be home from the service, her answer did have a bit of truth to it.

Randy had insisted she get to the juke joint early to take care of any last-minute preparations. Once the children were settled, he would ride to the club with Joe Frank.

"You nervous?" Bertha asked.

"What does she have to be nervous about?" Doreen replied as she slowly made her way toward the women. Cass was tempted to take bets on how long it would take the woman to fall out of her shoes. "She's been on stage before."

"There are many reasons to be nervous," Cass insisted. The main one was what she would do when Randy did arrive.

She could not in good conscience deny their relationship with him standing next to her. Yet the truth could cause a bucketload of problems for them.

****

"So how are things?"

Randy tensed at the question he had been dreading ever since his brother-in-law arrived on Friday. How was he supposed to tell the man he was in no position to support his sister and things did not look too promising in the near future?

Joe Frank stared straight ahead at the dark road. He maintained a light grip on the steering wheel. Neither his knuckles nor the vein in his temple protruded through skin.

While Randy preferred the idea of getting a healthy tooth extracted, he took a deep breath and followed the teaching of his mentor.

"I haven't found a job yet." He blurted out the confession, then snapped his mouth shut. He would not offer any excuses. Just like he would not want to hear any from his daughters' husbands, he was sure this man did not want to hear any either.

"Actually, that's not what I was asking," Joe Frank clarified. "I was curious about how things were going between Cass and you."

Having not expected that question, several seconds passed before Randy replied, "Everythin's fine."

"Good to know." Joe Frank turned his head till he had one eye on the road and one on Randy. "I noticed the tension between the two of you on Christmas."

It was just a week ago that Cass did not want him to touch her and he was starving for attention. But after the past few nights, her rejection was a distant memory.

Joe Frank turned his attention back to the road. "Just for the record, I don't think less of you for staying with your daughters. You're doing something to help out around the house, which is more than what many of the men I know would do."

"Give Me the Simple Life" rose over the crunch of tires rolling over the gravel. Randy leaned closer to his window, straining to hear Cass's rich voice belt out the lyrics of the second song in the set she'd planned.

Disappointment tugged at him. He had wanted to be present from the first note, offering her support when she made her return to the stage.

Joe Frank pulled into an empty spot between a black pickup and a blue convertible, and Randy climbed out of the coupe before his brother-in-law shifted into park.

Cass and the trumpeter held the last note of the song for four beats before abruptly ending the song. The crowd erupted in applause.

Envy replaced his disappointment. He should be the one accompanying Cass, not some stranger who did not understand that she expressed her emotions through her songs.

The upbeat numbers she started her performances with reflected her excitement at being in front of the audience. The more mellow songs were reserved for the end of the show to help her wind down and get ready for bed. And anytime she finished with "Dream a Little Dream of Me," the first song they had performed together, Randy knew they were going straight to bed but not necessarily straight to sleep when they got home.

Patrons who were lingering outside turned and gawked at him as he wove around one group and then sidestepped another to reach the entrance. Less than ten yards from his goal, a man whose fists looked like they would offer Joe Louis a challenge stepped into Randy's path.

"You lost?" His deep voice drowned out the murmurs of the spectators.

"I'm here to see the show," Randy replied. He peered around the man and caught a glimpse of Cass's royal blue evening gown. Unlike her sister-in-law, she'd kept her outfit simple, wearing a dress she had made two years earlier, wearing her hair in a French twist and topping it off with a string of pearls around her neck and teardrop earrings hanging from her lobes.

"It's cool, man," Joe Frank said, stopping behind him. "He's with me."

"You know that's not how things work around here." The man addressed Joe Frank as if Randy was not standing there.

"It's all right. He's—"

"A friend." Randy jumped in, hoping to avoid any possible conflicts that would come with revealing the truth. It was Cass's moment to shine, and he was not about to have them yanking her off the stage in the middle of a set because of him.

"Look, there are plenty of places in town where you can hang." The man pulled a wad of cash out of his pocket and peeled off five singles. "This should be enough to get you in the door and pay for a drink." He held out the money. "My treat."

"He don't need your damn money." Joe Frank knocked the man's hand back.

Randy grabbed his brother-in-law and pulled him back. "It's all right. Maybe I should go."

"This ain't right," Joe Frank protested.

Randy released his brother-in-law. "Maybe not, but it is what it is." It was not a reality he wanted to accept, but it was one he would abide by, that night. "Tell everyone I'll catch them later." He shoved his fists into his pants pockets and strolled back down the road.

As much as it pained him to walk away, it would have hurt even more to do something to ruin Cass's evening.

****

"Thank you." Cass raised her voice to be heard over the applause. "I want to wish everyone a Happy New Year and a good night. Please get home safely."

The cheers turned to pleas for another song. Cass, however, did not have it in her to perform one more second. She had sung for six hours, which was five hours and fifty minutes longer than her heart had been in it.

Despite her disappointment in having to take the stage without Randy in the audience, Cass was professional and started the show on time. However, she had been ready to walk off when Joe Frank strolled in without Randy. It was only his curt nod that made her continue.

"Cass, you were fantastic," Doreen shouted, moving toward the stage. "Listen to them. They want more."

"They're not getting it tonight," Cass commented as she stepped off the platform.

Zed rushed forward and motioned for the band to play another song. "You're not serious about leavin'."

"Our deal was for six hours." She held out her hand. "I kept my end of the bargain, now you'll keep yours."

The man's eyes narrowed. He stared at the extended limb. When it did not wither under his glare, he slowly slipped his hand inside his blazer as if the movement pained him.

"The crowd loved you, Miss Cass," he announced, pulling a billfold from his pocket. "You should consider comin' back."

"You even got the white people wantin' to hear you," Doreen added, slurring her words.

Cass turned to the woman by her side. "What are you talking about?" She crossed her arms over her chest.

"Heard some white man was tryin' to get in to see the show. But they turned him away at the door."

Cass glanced over the woman's head at Joe Frank. Her brother frowned and nodded, confirming the woman's version of the events.

Her temper flared. She should have known better. Wasn't she the one who had told Randy they could not be together in town? What made her think things would be different at the juke joint?

"So what do you say?" Zed's voice interrupted the internal rant Cass was having with herself.

"What?" She showed no remorse for not giving the man her undivided attention.

"You'll come back and sing?"

Hell, no!

Cass successfully swallowed her protest before it slipped from between her lips. It was too tempting to tell the man where he could stick his offer. Instead, she not only recalled her mother's teachings, she followed it.

She reached around her co-worker and accepted the coat Joe Frank held out to her. Without a word or a second glance at the siblings who had convinced her to ring in the New Year performing in an establishment where her husband was not welcomed, she marched to her car.

As she drove home, Cass fumed at her shortsightedness. She should have asked more questions about the juke joint's clientele. While it was obvious who frequented the establishment, she could have inquired whether management was willing to extend an invitation to others.

Silence greeted Cass as she pulled up behind the garage. A lone light shone in the window in the front of the apartment. The amber glow from the cigarette illuminated the face she had been longing to see all night.

"How'd you do?" he called from his perch on the second to last step as she climbed out of the car.

"What do you think?"

"That they asked you to return for a twelve-week engagement and they're goin' to pay you twenty dollars a night."

Cass walked to the building and stopped in front of

him. "You're very optimistic. Just like I was."

He dropped the cigarette on the ground and mashed the butt with his heel. "You don't need to apologize." He reached out, wrapped his fingers around hers, and pulled her between his legs.

"But I should've known...I should've asked." She settled on his knee and encircled her arms around his neck.

"In that apartment, we're in our own little world. Sometimes it's easy to forget there's another world out there and not everyone's as acceptin' as we are."

"I prefer our world. Can't we just stay there and forget about..." She waved a hand at the trees.

"I wish we could. In fact, I'd prefer it." He pulled her hand back to his neck. "But then I look at you and remember not every encounter's disastrous."

Cass humphed. She wished she could be as optimistic as he was. At times if felt like everyone she met was against them.

"So did you agree to perform there again?"

"After I learned you were turned away, I walked without getting paid." She brushed aside a strand of hair that fell over his forehead. "But even if they had let you in to see the show, I can't break up the act."

She leaned down and brushed her lips over his. He reached up and stroked his finger across her cheek.

"What song did you end with?"

" 'Moonlight Becomes You.' "

"I was hopin' you'd end with 'Dream a Little Dream of Me.' "

"I planned to...during a private performance," she whispered, before leaning in for a deeper and longer kiss.

Chapter 12

Randy was in deep shit.

The glint in Shara's eye indicated she had tucked away his curse for future use at a family gathering or while shaking hands with her grandmother's pastor after church. That, however, did not bother him as much as Sylvia's O-shaped mouth. The girl was going to reveal his transgression before Cass cleared the threshold.

At least with Shara, he would be able to pretend he did not know where she picked up the language. But how would he be able to deny the truth when Cass glanced from Sylvia to him, silently questioning the girl's version of the afternoon.

"You really don't have to tell your mother about this, do you?"

His eldest nodded.

Randy's head dropped forward. He could almost taste Mother Porter's lye soap and hear the disappointment in her voice as she lectured him on the importance of showing restraint around the girls. As far as the woman would be concerned, there was no excuse for vulgarity. Even a missing ingredient for the cake he was making did not excuse the harsh language.

They were a week into the New Year, and Randy still sensed Cass's disappointment at him being turned away from her show. He had, therefore, decided to bake a cake to cheer her up. While he knew the sweets would not solve their problems, it would be a nice distraction.

He had already mixed the dry ingredients and had added the eggs and water when he discovered they were out of butter. He had meant to pick up some at the market that morning. The trip, however, had been cut short after Sylvia announced her need to visit the facilities.

Randy had left a half-filled basket in the store with the intention of returning to complete the chore after he took his daughter to the restroom. But the moment he saw the dank, moldy closet reserved for coloreds, he decided to abandon the basket and return home.

Shara dipped a finger in the bowl and licked the batter from the digit. Her twisted lips would have made Randy laugh had he not been planning to assure Sylvia's silence with the promise of an extra slice of the finished product.

"I got your mail," Mr. Johnston announced as he opened the door.

Randy prayed the man could offer advice on how to distract Cass from the tale of his slip of the tongue or help fix his cake.

The girls slid out of the chairs they had been kneeling on, ran to the man, and each threw her arms around one of his legs. Randy clenched his fists against the bout of jealousy that surged through him.

How could the girls warm up to the man they had only known for two weeks, yet still hesitate to come near him? Forget the cake; he needed something a bit stronger to get over his disappointment.

"Where'd you like me to put these?" Mr. Johnston waved the three envelopes in the air.

"Sylvia will take them." Randy felt no need to sort through the mail, as he had received his monthly letter from Miss Sylvia, the only person he corresponded with, a week earlier.

Mr. Johnston passed the letters to the girl, who took off to her parents' bedroom to place the envelopes on Cass's side of the dresser. Shara released her hold on the man to tag behind her sister, though it would only take the older girl less than a minute to complete the chore.

Randy snatched the mixing bowl off the table and headed into the kitchen.

"Whatcha got there?" Mr. Johnston asked.

"From the expression on Shara's face, slop."

Mr. Johnston walked over to Randy and stuck his finger in the bowl. He tasted the mixture, then nodded his head.

"Needs butter and vanilla."

"Damn," Randy muttered. Vanilla was also on the list he had left in the basket with the groceries.

In no mood to run all over town looking for a store that stocked the groceries he needed and had facilities that he would not mind his daughters using, Randy decided to abandon his project. He walked over by the sink and depressed the lever on the garbage can, popping open the lid.

"Don't pour that out."

"It's not like I got the ingredients to fix this."

"Come downstairs. I'm sure I got what your need."

Randy set the bowl on the side of the sink. He glanced back at the girls, who had just stepped out of the bedroom.

"Y'all go sit over there and play with your dolls."

He pointed to the table and the doll clothes he had pushed to the side to mix the cake. "I'll be back in a minute."

He waited until the girls had scrambled into their chairs before he followed the man downstairs. Mr. Johnston strolled into the store and to a door in the rear.

"Come in." He waved Randy into the saddest room that ever existed.

Unmade cots sat on both sides of the door. In the middle of the floor was a crate with two stools on either side. A hot plate sat on top of the icebox in the far corner of the room.

Shame filled Randy as he remembered his criticism of the apartment above the little room. While his living quarters were not what he had grown used to over the years, it was a hell of a lot better than what their landlord had settled for.

"After my wife died and my son moved on to start his own family, I didn't see the need for all that space up there," Mr. Johnston explained as if he could read Randy's mind. "Figured it'd be more useful to a young couple starting out."

"What about your grandson?"

"Boy don't care one way or the other." He pointed to the stove with one hand as he opened the icebox with the other. "As long as he gets a story each night and wakes up to bacon and eggs each morning, he's fine."

Randy recalled when simply waking up to a hot breakfast would make his day. He wouldn't care that he had to untangle himself from the blankets he had spread underneath him to cushion the floor where he'd slept the previous evening. Nor was he concerned that the floor was in a one-room house that had neither indoor plumbing nor electricity.

He wondered when that was suddenly not enough. At the moment, he now had a wife, who was honoring her vows to stick with him "for poorer." And he had his daughters, who seemed content as long as they had their dolls and a story each night. So why did it bother him that they were not living in a city apartment with the most modern conveniences?

As if his maker wanted to find the most bone-chilling way to answer his question, a screech drifted from upstairs. Ignoring the butter Mr. Johnston held out to him, Randy dashed out of the building, around the side, and up the stairs, taking two steps at a time.

Sylvia jumped back from the bathroom door as he burst into the apartment. The sound of running water blended with her sister's screams.

Randy rushed into the room, where Shara stood on the stool, cradling her red hand to her chest. Tears ran down her cheeks as she continued to scream.

Randy turned off the water, snatched the girl from the stool, and with her tucked under his arm, he raced to her bedroom.

"Put this on," he said, pulling Sylvia's coat out of the closet.

As the girl obeyed, he draped Shara's coat over her shoulders. He grabbed the car keys from the peg near the door and ran back downstairs.

"What happened?" Mr. Johnston asked, opening the car door.

"She burnt her hand on the damn water," Randy replied, with no concern about his language or the young ears taking in every word he uttered. "Where's the closest doctor?" He ducked into the car and placed

Shara into the front seat.

"You'll do better drivin' her to Norfolk Community."

"Ain't nothin' closer?" While Randy did not have anything against the colored hospital, he did not want to waste the extra minutes it would take to get there if someone was closer.

The man hesitated.

Randy stepped out of the car and faced his landlord. He could read the man's internal debate. "Where is he?"

"Down the road," Mr. Johnston pointed in the direction opposite of town. "But he ain't too friendly with coloreds," he confessed.

"She's only half-colored."

"He ain't gonna see it that way."

Randy knew most people did not care whether the girl was one hundred percent, fifty percent, or twenty-five percent colored. One drop of colored blood made her colored and subject to the same scorn as everyone else who was colored.

Randy glanced down at Sylvia, who stood between the two men and stared at him. "Get in." As she climbed into the car next to her sister, he turned back to the man. "Where is he?"

Mr. Johnston growled, "Make a left at the first turn and go up one block. It's the house on the northeast corner."

Randy checked to make sure both girls were completely inside the car before he slammed the door closed.

"I don't know whatcha tryin' to prove, but you shouldn't drag them into this," Mr. Johnston called out

Bitter Blues

as Randy sprinted to the driver's side. "They're just kids."

A voice in his head, which sounded remarkably like Mother Porter's, echoed the sentiment. It then added, "There's enough trouble out there. Don't go lookin' for more."

Ignoring the advice from both of his elders, Randy climbed into the car and drove toward the doctor's office. His daughter was injured. Surely the doctor would be willing to put aside his stupid prejudices for the sake of a child.

Randy parked across the street from the white house. A sign advertising the doctor's name swung from two chains attached to the roof over the porch.

Ignoring a second sign posted in the lawn that pointed toward the rear of the house, he ran up the steps and nudged opened the front door with his foot.

"I need a doctor," he announced, running into the waiting room with Shara in one arm and Sylvia clinging to his other hand.

The two mothers sitting in the waiting room grabbed their children and recoiled from Randy as if his family were carrying a contagious disease.

The nurse, whose tight bun contributed to her harsh expression, jumped out of her chair. "Get them out of here." Her massive girth jiggled underneath her white uniform.

"You don't understand. She's hurt." He released Sylvia's hand and patted Shara's back.

"And you don't understand. We have rules. You want them seen, you go round back to the colored entrance."

"What difference does it make which entrance I go

through? She's just as injured over here as she'll be back there."

"What's all the yelling out here?" A gray-haired man wearing brown pants and a white coat over his white dress shirt and brown plaid tie stepped from the room in the back. "This is a doctor's office, not a playground."

"He refused to go round back," the nurse replied.

"She burnt her hand," Randy said. "She needs medical attention."

"She'll be seen after you take her around back, where coloreds belong," the doctor stated.

"She's half-white. Doesn't that mean anything?"

"It means you need to be more discriminating about who you sleep with." The doctor's upper lip pulled back, his forehead wrinkled and his nostrils flared. "Now, get those pickaninnies out of here." He shoved Sylvia's shoulder.

When Randy's vision cleared, the doctor was pinned against the wall. A fistful of the man's shirt was enclosed in Randy's hands. Shara stood on the nurse's desk, where he figured he must have set her before grabbing the other man. Sylvia sat on the floor, watching him with wide eyes.

The shrieks from the parents scrambling toward the door could not drown out the vile name echoing in Randy's mind.

"They're the most precious angels you'll ever have the pleasure to meet. And you'll give them the respect they deserve."

"Get out," the man gasped.

"With pleasure." He pulled the man forward then slammed him back, relishing the sound of his head smacking the wall.

Randy released the man. He bent down, picked up Sylvia, and dropped her on one hip. He then placed Shara on the other hip.

"You come back here, and I'll call the police," the nurse threatened, moving to her boss's side.

"You won't have to worry about that," Randy tossed over his shoulder as he marched out. He spat on the sign he had ignored when he rushed to the office.

Once the girls were settled in the car, he climbed into the driver's seat and pulled away from the curb. His ears caught the faint sound of sirens in the distance. Though he was certain the doctor could not have summoned the police that quickly, he did not want to stick around in case his theory was wrong.

As he made a right at the corner, he caught a glimpse of the girls. The distress in their eyes said the curses he'd uttered earlier would be the least of his worries that evening.

****

"I wish you'd reconsider singing at the juke joint," Doreen said, setting a drill on the tool cart. "I'm sure Zed would consider paying you more."

"It ain't the money," Cass mumbled to the persistent request her co-worker had been making since the New Year's performance. She did not bother to mention that Zed had never paid her for the hours she had already provided.

"I know Zed's Palace is not what you're used to, but we're fixing it up, making it more classy." Doreen snatched the rag from the cart as Bertha reached for the cloth. "And I promise we won't have any more trespassers."

Cass shuddered at the term the woman used to refer to Randy.

"I just don't understand them." Doreen tossed the rag on the cart, ignoring Bertha's outstretched hand. "It's not enough that they got places we can't visit, now they're trying to intrude on our territory."

Cass's shoulders ached from the guilt that weighed down on her. She had promised before the justice of the peace and friends to "love and cherish" Randy. Yet in order to hold onto a job, she refused to speak up for him.

"You need to let it go," Bertha said as she set her sandwich on the red bandanna she spread across her lap.

"How can I, after he come strutting to the juke joint like he owned the place?" Doreen asked.

"How do you know he was struttin'? You were too busy pickin' yourself off the floor after fallin' in those shoes you were prancin' around in."

Doreen ducked her head. "I just know, that's all. I'm curious as to who invited him. I wouldn't be surprised if it was Martha Lynn. I'm sure she likes her meat on the light side."

Cass slammed her lunchbox on the cart. Bertha jumped, and Doreen's head snapped up.

"You should take Bertha's advice and shut your mouth about things you don't know." Before either woman could reply, she marched away.

With no particular destination in mind, Cass continued walking until the cold air jerked her back to reality. A cluster of men hanging around a truck whistled and offered to help her find her way.

"Y'all hush your mouths and get back to work,"

Bertha called over her shoulder before grabbing Cass's arm.

The men ceased their catcalls and insulted the women with references to their appearance and their preference in partners.

The women ignored the men and continued around the building.

"Shame all they need is that thing hangin' between their legs to call themselves men." Bertha sucked her teeth. "Hate to put them in the same category as my Angelo."

"Momma used to say, 'You can call a pig a ballerina, but it don't make it so,' " Cass replied.

Her companion stopped walking and laughed. "I love that. Tell your momma I'm gonna start usin' that."

"She'll be happy to know someone likes her sayings."

"I'm curious to know what she had to say about you and your man." The woman wiped away the tears rolling down her cheek with the back of her hand.

"What do you mean?"

"I mean no one visited D.C. without stoppin' at the Panama Lounge to see Randy and Cass."

Her mouth dropped open at the mention of the venue where she and Randy had performed for the four years they lived in the city. "Wh…wh…why—"

"A woman who never has a problem holdin' her tongue didn't say anythin'?"

Cass nodded. She knew she looked ridiculous with her mouth hanging open and her head bobbing up and down. However, her appearance was her last concern.

"You're a good worker. What benefit would there've been in revealin' the truth? All that would've done is made you the topic on everyone's tongue."

"You knew who he was when he came here looking for a job?"

Bertha nodded. "I visited my sister at least once a year, and I saw the show each time." She placed a hand on Cass's shoulder. "Don't know why y'all chose to come down here instead of stayin' in the north, but as long as you're here, know you've at least one ally."

Cass's shoulders felt lighter knowing someone else was not only privy to her secret but the consequence had not been as traumatic as she had imagined.

****

From the scowl on Randy's face, Cass knew she was not going to like the answer to her nightly inquiry about his day. Hoping for a few minutes to unwind before she had to deal with whatever problem had arisen, she glanced around the room for the girls.

"Where's Sylvia and Shara?"

"I put them to bed early," he replied, taking her lunchbox from her. "They missed their naps today."

"Why?" she asked, slipping out of her coat.

"Shara had an accident."

A chill coursed through Cass. With her coat hanging off one arm, she raced to the girls' bedroom. She threw open the door, yet neither girl stirred.

Her gaze dropped to the white bandage covering Shara's hand, which rested on top of the blanket.

"What happened?"

"She burnt her hand on the hot water."

His voice was full of remorse as he related the events leading up to the accident. "I shouldn't have left them by themselves."

A part of her wanted to agree with him, but his

drooping shoulders indicated he was already riddled with guilt. Adding more to his distress was not going to do any of them any good.

"What did the doctor say?"

"They cleaned her hand and applied an ointment before bandagin' it," Randy replied, taking her coat from her. "They gave me a tube of the ointment and extra bandages."

Cass tiptoed to the bed, leaned over, and kissed both girls on the forehead. She adjusted the blankets around them before returning to his side.

"You did good," Cass reassured him, stroking his arm. "She'll be fine."

"There's more." His tone became graver.

Her hand dropped to her side. Fear gripped her and squeezed until she thought she would suffocate.

"She's gonna lose her hand?"

"No." He lightly touched the small of her back and led her to the table. He pulled out a chair and waved toward it.

"What's going on?" She sat on the edge of her seat.

Randy tossed her coat across the table. He crouched in front of her, took her hand and continued the story from the time he left the apartment. Once the additional details were revealed, anger had replaced her fears.

She snatched her hands from his. "What were you thinkin', takin' my girls to that man?" she screamed, unable and unwilling to keep her voice down.

"That *my* baby was hurt and she needed a doctor," he replied.

"He was the last man you should've gone to."

Though Norfolk Community was farther away and

the fee was a bit more than the doctor's, everyone she knew preferred the medical facility over the man. Those who visited him were forced to wait for hours in a shed that barely offered protection from the rain and none from the cold. When he finally got to the coloreds, he would tell them to stick out the affected body parts, which he would proceed to examine from a distance of no less than two feet. He would then bark instructions on how to tend to the problem before demanding they drop his fee in a basket by the door on their way out.

"You would've done better takin' her to a witch doctor who lights fires and dances around while chantin' oogadie-boogadie-boo."

"I know that now."

He reached for her hand. Too angry to want his touch, Cass slipped out of the chair and jumped out of his reach. She pressed her fists into her side so as not to give in to the temptation to pound on his chest.

"Just 'cause *you* choose to look beyond a person's skin color, it doesn't mean others are goin' to be just as acceptin'."

"I realize that." Randy stood up. His eyes shone from the pain of her rejection, yet he did not move toward her. "I just thought…" He turned his head from her.

When he failed to complete the sentence, Cass asked, "You thought what? That he'd ignore Shara's colored half and treat the white part?"

Though he nodded his head, he refused to look at her.

"You better get used to the fact that your daughters are colored and the world's not gonna treat them differently 'cause their father's white. Maybe one day things will be different, but for the time bein', they're gonna be pointed to the colored entrance, denied service, and treated like second-class citizens."

"I don't like it."

"And you think I enjoy it?"

Randy held out his hand. Cass hesitated a heartbeat before she forced herself to step into his embrace. She felt the protection and comfort he had to offer. And though the embrace did not make everything right, it felt good to know he was there for her…for them.

"This is my reality and your daughters' reality. And you'll have to make it a part of your reality so you can help prepare them for the future." She wrapped her arms around his waist and laid her head on his chest, offering him as much comfort as he offered her.

That afternoon she had discovered she was not totally alone at the shipyard. But for every one person who couldn't give a fig about them being together, there would be twice as many people against them. They would need to support each other if they hoped to get through it.

Chapter 13

The attack had come without warning.

Randy's hands covered his groin. Flashes of light obscured his vision as pain radiated from his core to the tips of each extremity. His brain cried for the future children he would not be able to produce.

He rolled from his attacker, but there was nowhere safe for him to go. His body hovered in the air for less than a second before it slammed to the floor.

A soft murmur inquired about his well-being. Before he could grunt his reply, a snore told him just how worried the woman was about his distress.

Randy lay on the floor until he was certain his shaky limbs could support his weight. He rolled onto his hands and knees and peered over the side of the bed. His head jerked as the small foot shot forward and grazed his temple.

His addled brain tried to figure out how Sylvia and Shara managed to crawl into the bed without waking either parent. The strain from the chore only succeeded in making his head hurt. After a minute, he gave up his quest to find a logical explanation and decided to find some place safe to spend the rest of the night.

Randy pushed to his feet and stumbled to the chair where he had draped his pants before climbing under the covers with Cass. He pulled his pants over his boxers, then shuffled out of the bedroom to the girls' room. In the dim glow from the moon, he made out the discarded nightgown on the floor and the opened dresser drawer with clothes precariously hanging over the side.

Even half asleep, Randy was able to conclude from the turmoil that an accident had sent the girls fleeing to a dry bed.

In no mood to deal with the mess, he backed out of the room and headed for the sofa. The wooden frame creaked as he stretched out on the cushions. His head perched on one armrest as his feet dangled over the other. Without a doubt, this sleeping arrangement would cause a crick or two in his body. That, however, was preferable to another mind-numbing blow to the crotch.

Randy pulled over him the blanket he kept draped over the back of the sofa for the girls' midday nap, rolled onto his side, and was ready to welcome sleep when a murmur caught his attention. Before he could contemplate why he heard voices, the door flew open.

****

Cass shot up in the bed at the sound of a door slamming open.

"Randy?" she called out as the girls ducked behind her. "What's going on?"

The bedroom door flew open and smacked the wall behind it. She shrieked and the girls whimpered, their small bodies trembling against hers.

"Get out here." The stranger stepped into the doorway and barked the order.

Before she could comply, another man stormed into the room. He grabbed her arm and dragged her out of the bed. Sylvia and Shara clung to each other with one hand and reached for her with their other.

Their cries tore at Cass's heart. Unable to go to them, she had never felt so helpless before in her life.

Cass stumbled as her captor dragged her barefoot through the door. With his iron grip on her arm, she feared the limb would snap in two if she failed to keep up with him.

"Get off her," Randy ordered as she was yanked into the living room. The gun pointing at him prevented him coming to her aid. "What are you doin'?"

The light over the kitchen table flickered on. The uniforms worn by the intruders identified them of members of Norfolk's police department.

A round, balding man stepped forward and announced, "It has been brought to the attention of the Norfolk Police Department that an illegal cohabitation is taking place on these premises." He wiped the beads of sweat from his forehead. "The complaint was filed by a Dr. Anderson. He said a white man burst into his office with two colored girls."

Cass bristled at the accusation. Though she was curious as to how they could have traced Randy back to the apartment, she was more concerned about how they would get out of the situation unscathed.

While she had always expected a nasty look or a rude comment regarding her marriage when she was in public, she had always considered her house a safe haven. She had never imagined someone would break down her door, drag her from her bed, and threaten her children.

"Mrs. Porter, is everythin' all right up there?" Mr. Johnston called from below. The tapping from a pair of soft-soled shoes grew louder until the man stepped into the doorway, wearing a green flannel bathrobe over a matching pair of pajamas and the brown bedroom slippers Cass had given him for Christmas. "What's goin' on?"

"Who are you?" demanded the man who had announced the complaint against Randy and Cass.

"Albert Johnston. I own the business downstairs and this house." He glanced across the room. "What's goin' on? Who are you?" He nodded in Randy's direction.

Remembering his promise not to intervene if trouble came to their door, Cass was certain the man was denying all knowledge of her relationship with Randy. And while she had not expected someone to take on their problems, she was disappointed at the betrayal.

"Randy Jones."

The older man's brow wrinkled for a second, before he smiled. "You're the young man my son wrote me about."

"You know this man?" The official asked.

"He saved my son's life overseas. My boy would've been run over if this young man hadn't pushed him outta the way of a Jeep." Mr. Johnston turned back to Randy. "I thought you had another three months before they let you go."

Mr. Johnston was so convincing, for a second Cass believed that Randy and the man's son actually knew each other. But Randy had never left the States.

Too afraid the police would see through the lie and take them all in, Cass held her breath as the men continued their ruse.

"Got out early," Randy replied.

"What are you doing here?" The lawman barked.

"My son told him to drop by if he needed anythin' after he was discharged," Mr. Johnston replied.

"I got into town yesterday and you weren't home. Your tenant was kind enough to offer me the sofa." Randy pointed to the blanket that lay half on the sofa and half on the floor.

"Dr. Anderson said this man burst into his office with two colored girls, claiming they were his."

"Must've thought he'd be helpin' by doin' so," Mr. Johnston suggested. "He's from up north and don't understand how things are done down here."

Cass prayed the men did not listen too closely to Randy's accent and realize he was also born and raised in the South.

Another officer strolled out of the girls' room. "The bed in here smells like piss," he announced. "Must belong to her pickaninnies."

She noticed Randy's jaw tighten. His hands balled into fists. She mentally willed him to bite his tongue.

The police officer glanced around the room as if searching for any evidence to dispute their claims. His gaze locked on the olive-green duffel bag Randy had filled with clothes the girls had overgrown and placed on the floor by the door so he could remember to drop them off at Goodwill in the morning. The overcoat slung over the back of the dining chair and the size-ten men's shoes lying in the middle of the floor added believability to the lie. For once Cass was grateful for Randy's habit of leaving his shoes wherever he kicked them off.

The lawman finally stared at the dog tags Randy continued to wear around his neck out of habit. "Let 'em go," he said.

The officer released his grip on Cass's arm. She stepped to the side, allowing the man who had been blocking the children from her to pass.

"Now that you're home, I'm sure your son's friend will make other arrangements for accommodation."

"Of course," Mr. Johnston said. "I'm sorry for all the trouble we've caused, Mrs. Porter."

Randy shoved his feet into his shoes, then grabbed his coat and bag. "Thank you for your hospitality, ma'am," he said, before stepping out of the apartment.

One by one, the men filed out behind him. Once all the footsteps had faded, Cass pushed the battered door back in place and ran into the bedroom.

Sylvia and Shara reached out to Cass. She, however, could not gather the girls into her arms and reassure them everything would be all right. The apartment no longer felt like home…it was no longer a place she could go to feel safe and comforted.

She dropped to her knees and reached under the bed until her hand touched the handle of her suitcase. She dragged it out and placed it on top of the sheets.

As she snatched clothes from the closet and tossed them into the suitcase, she vowed to make it up to the girls once they were at the one place where she always felt secure.

Chapter 14

"We need a place to stay."

The words Cass had never expected to utter to her parents left a bitter taste in her mouth. Even after her first husband left her in New York with no job and no place to lay her head, she had managed to bounce back and make it on her own. However, with two children to protect, she couldn't simply throw the dice and see what sides the fates offered her. The girls needed stability and, more important, a safe environment.

Her mother glanced past her to the car loaded with all their possessions.

"I'll send your father out to help," the older woman replied. "Is your husband stayin'?"

Cass peered over her shoulder at Randy, who was pulling bags from the back of the vehicle. "I haven't decided."

That morning, she had been tempted to load up the car and drive away without so much as a "nay" to him. But when he came around the corner as she shoved the last bag into the back seat, some of her anger faded.

The stress lines marring his forehead and the worry in his eyes indicated his night had been as restless as hers. Yes, it was his actions that had led the police to their door. But he had not reacted out of malice. He had done so out of genuine concern for his daughter.

In her desire to put as much space between Norfolk

and herself, Cass had not bothered to drive by the shipyard to give official notice or collect what was owed to her. She only thanked Mr. Johnston for his assistance and handed over an envelope with what she hoped would be enough to cover all the damages caused by the police.

"Have y'all eaten?" her mother asked.

"Not yet."

"Take the girls to the kitchen and fix 'em some breakfast."

Cass herded Sylvia and Shara through the house to the other building while her mother stuck her head into the bedroom to announce they would have guests for a few days. She pointed to the table, and the girls scrambled into the chairs while she gathered the ingredients to make a pot of mush.

"Feel free to slam that around if you need to," her mother said as Cass placed the cast-iron pot on the stove. "As many times as I've come in here after your father's made me mad, I can assure you that's not gonna break."

After the rude awakening the girls had earlier, Cass did not think they needed to hear her slamming around the kitchen. However, sending them off with their grandfather so she could work out her frustrations while she made dinner later seemed like a good idea.

"What happened?" her mother asked.

The concern in the woman's voice broke the dam Cass had erected to hold back her tears.

"Good lord, you're tremblin'." Her mother placed a half loaf of banana bread on the table. "Sylvia, you and your sister share this." She draped an arm around Cass's shoulder and steered her out of the building.

"What happened?" She sat on the top step and pointed to the space beside her.

Despite the nippy morning air, Cass sat next to the older woman. It took a moment of fighting her emotions before she could relay the details of Randy's visit to the doctor's office and the subsequent visit from the police in the middle of the night.

"Good thin' your landlord's able to think fast on his feet. No tellin' what would've happened had he not come up with that lie."

Cass shuddered at the thought she had been trying not to entertain after everyone left the apartment. Who would have looked after her girls if the police had insisted she and Randy accompany them to the station?

"I'm sorry you had to go through that, but at least y'all got through it."

"I'm not sure about that," Cass mumbled, picking at a speck of lint on her skirt.

Her mother placed a hand over hers. "I know you're upset, but take a day or two before you make any decisions. You don't wanna regret anythin' you do in anger."

"But I don't think I'm ever going to get over last night."

Her heart raced whenever she remembered being dragged out of bed. The fear threatened to choke her.

"You were scared...you're still scared. But you gotta remember that you took Randy for better and for worse. And you knew before you recited your vows that it wasn't always gonna be easy."

"But I never knew he was going to chase after danger."

"I'll admit, takin' Shara to that doctor wasn't the

brightest move, but you must remember he did it with the best intentions." Her mother echoed the sentiment she had repeated to herself during the drive to Piney Woods to keep from pulling to the side of the road and ordering Randy out of the car. "No matter how bad you feel right now, I'm sure your husband feels ten times worse. He loves you and the girls and would never want harm to come to y'all."

While everything her mother said was true, Cass still found his actions hard to accept.

****

He'd fucked up big time.

Though his father-in-law did not make a habit of using profanity, the frown on his dark brown face did not mince words. Not that Randy disagreed with the sentiment.

He had made a colossal mess in not just his life but the lives of those he loved. In only twenty-four hours, his actions had nearly got him and Cass arrested, caused her to lose her job, and made them homeless.

"I'm sorry I disappointed you, sir," Randy said to break the silence that followed his explanation as to why his family was moving back to the farm.

"You didn't disappoint me," the older man replied. His dark brown eyes were cold with anger. "I expected somethin' crazy from you. Just figured it'd happen sooner than it did."

While Cass's mother had welcomed him into the family, he knew her father had not warmed up to the idea that Randy was married to his daughter or was the father of his grandchildren. Yet he would never have guessed that the man's dislike for him extended that deep.

"No matter how much you think you understand what we go through, you'll never truly know. And it's because of that you'll take risks that can backfire on you."

"Mack, that's enough," Mother Porter announced as she stepped onto the front porch. "Cassie Ann is in the bedroom tryin' to find places to put everythin'. Why don't you see if the girls saved you some banana bread?"

The man towered over his wife. If he had chosen not to comply, there was nothing she could have done to make him. Yet without so much as a grumble, he placed the bag he pulled from the back of the car onto the ground and shuffled around to the back of the house.

"You'll have to excuse him," Mother Porter said, walking toward the car.

"No reason to apologize for the truth."

He had never been under any illusion that he understood all the hardships Cass had experienced. He could walk into practically any store or restaurant and not turn heads. It was his mistake for forgetting that the privilege would not be extended to his family when they were with him.

The woman stopped by his side and crossed her arms over her chest. "So what were you thinkin'?"

During the drive from Norfolk, Cass had blurted out the question more than once. However, her hard glare on the road and her clenched jaw said she was venting and did not expect…or want…an answer.

The questioning glint in his mother-in-law's eyes, and her rigid stance, indicated hers was not a rhetorical question. She expected not only an answer but a satisfactory one, at that.

"I was thinkin' that I was mindin' my own business, enjoyin' my wife and family, when some uncle who never gave a damn about me before decided I needed to fight for freedom." He snorted. "What a joke. I don't have the freedom to walk down the street with my wife. Hell, my babies don't have the freedom to go to a doctor."

The scowl on the woman's face faded. Concern, understanding, and sympathy took its place. "Ironic, isn't it? You serve so other people are ensured the freedoms many of us can only dream of in this country." She sighed. "Every time the doctor told me I was with child, I had to question how we could bring another one into this world. Mack had a hell of a time teachin' the boys to hold their heads high with pride, despite someone always tryin' to bring 'em down. Whenever they went out, someone was ready to treat 'em like they were less of a man. And as for Cassie Ann…" The woman slowly moved her head from side to side. "I worried someone would try and take her 'cause they didn't see her as a woman but an object there for his amusement."

Mother Porter addressed concerns that plagued Randy whenever he heard a white man talk down to a colored man or remembered the crude comments other men in his unit made about colored women when they returned from leave.

"These past weeks, you proved you could be a father. Now you need to be the father of your colored children."

****

Randy perched on the stool Mother Porter used

when milking the cow and opened the case he had set at his feet. While the barn animals were not the most ideal audience, they weren't the worst crowd he'd ever played for.

He assembled the saxophone and played a medley of songs Cass and he had performed together when they lived in Harlem. At the time, their feelings for each other were new. There had been the hope of a future with her, despite her reservations. But now...even he had his doubts.

Would Cass be able to forgive him and allow them to move forward? More importantly, would he ever forgive himself and trust that he could do right for his family?

As he began playing "Sentimental Journey," Sylvia peeped around the corner. When she was younger, she would not settle down for her naps unless he serenaded her with lullabies. At that time, there was no question that she was Daddy's girl, but now...she gave him just as much respect as she would the clerk in the store.

When the song was over, he played "When You Wish Upon a Star."

Curiosity replaced the guarded look in her eyes. She stepped into the barn and inched her way to his side. Though he was certain she had been too young to remember him playing for her, a part of him hoped she recalled the times when it was just the two of them...a devoted father willing to do anything for his precious daughter.

Randy finished the song and lowered the saxophone. Instead of scurrying away, Sylvia stared up at him.

"Your momma send you to get me?"

She shook her head.

His disappointment was short-lived as it slowly sank in that the child had come to him on her own.

"You like the music?"

She nodded.

"You wanna hear more?"

Another nod.

He would have preferred she spoke up. However at that moment, he would settle for what she gave. She had taken a big step that day by coming to him. The lesson on making sure her voice was heard could wait another day.

Randy placed the reed to his lips. Cass's voice reached over the first note. Though he wanted to spend more time with his daughter, the concern in the woman's tone prompted him to lower the saxophone.

"Go on, your momma's callin' you. I'll play for you another time."

"Promise?" Despite the events of the previous night, her voice still held the innocence of youth.

Randy could not breathe around the lump in his throat. It was the first word she had spoken to him since his return without being prompted by others or by a disaster.

"Yes, I promise."

Sylvia threw her arms around his neck and placed a wet kiss on his cheek. He wrapped his arms around his daughter and held her close.

As far as Randy was concerned, only a coldhearted bastard could look at her sweet face or listen to the hope in her voice and not fall in love. He would learn how to protect her and her sister from those who could not recognize her beauty…both inside and out.

Chapter 15

The expletive slipped from Cass a second before the cup hit the floor and milk splattered a yard in every direction. It was the third dish Cass had dropped while clearing the table, in addition to the food she'd spilt while serving the girls during the course of the meal. Yet it was the profanity that troubled Randy.

While Cass was not a saint, she would not curse in front of her mother unless she was out of sorts.

"Somethin' botherin' you, girl?" her father asked.

"No, I'm fine." She snatched up the cup and disappeared into the kitchen.

His eyes narrowed, conveying his disbelief. He opened his mouth, then stopped and shook his head before hustling after Sylvia and Shara, who were waiting on the porch to go on their after-dinner walk.

"You're lookin' tired," Mother Porter called after her. "You been gettin' enough sleep?"

"Yes, Momma, I have." Cass stepped back into the room; her gaze focused on the mess. One did not need to see the guilt on her face to know she lied. Dark circles surrounded her eyes, she had become clumsy, and she snapped at the slightest provocation.

For over a week her tossing and turning had kept Randy awake. When she could no longer remain confined to one location, she wandered into the front room and hovered over the girls, who slept on the sofa.

Randy's chair scraped the floor as he pushed back from the table. He walked over to Cass and reached for the rag she carried. "I'll clean it up."

She snatched her hand out of his reach. "I got it." She knelt next to the mess.

At a loss for what to do, he could only stand over her and watch. How was he supposed to honor his vows to help in her time of need when she resisted all his attempts?

A gentle touch on his shoulder turned his attention to Mother Porter. Her eyes conveyed her sympathy. "Why don't you go for a walk? Have a cigarette." She squeezed his shoulder, silently informing him she wasn't offering him a choice.

With a sigh, he complied with the woman's wishes, reasoning his wife could not stay mad at him forever…at least, he hoped.

****

"Cassie Ann, I wanna talk to you—"

"I'm sorry for that slip," Cass mumbled. "It won't happen again."

"I'd appreciate that in the future, but that ain't what I wanted to talk about."

Cass sat back on her heels. "You want to talk about Randy," she said, listening to his shoes drag through the dirt.

He was hurting, possibly more than her. At least she had the support of her family to help her get through the tough times. All he got was an occasional comforting pat from her mother and an extra slice of cake.

She wished she could go after him…she wanted to. But her anger was too great. All she would do when she caught up with him would be to yell until she was hoarse.

Her mother shook her head. "I never messed in y'all's marriage, and I'm not about to start."

"Then what do you need to talk about?"

"Your new habit of lyin' to me."

Cass opened her mouth to protest.

Her mother continued, "Any fool can see you ain't been sleepin'." The older woman crouched in front of her. "What's goin' on?"

Cass did not know why she had lied to her mother. After staring at her ragged appearance in the mirror that morning, she knew she would not get through the day without being questioned.

"I'm afraid to close my eyes at night," she confessed, figuring it would be easier to tell the truth and get the lecture over with. "Every time I do, I hear my girls crying."

"What did Randy say when you told him?"

She shook her head. Since she had not told him, he had not said anything.

"You're stayin' up all night, not talkin' to Randy—you're destroyin' yourself and your family." Her mother rested a hand on her shoulder. "You need to talk to your husband. Comfort him and let him comfort you before he turns to someone else for what you should've been offerin' him."

For someone who didn't mess in people's marriage, her mother had a lot of advice. And as usual, that advice made a lot of sense.

****

The hush that hung in the air proved silence was golden.

For half an hour, Randy had tried to produce a sound that came close to music, but with his heart not into what he was doing, he only irritated the animals. When he could no longer tolerate their snorts, groans, and other sounds of protest, he pulled the saxophone from his mouth and proceeded to disassemble the instrument.

"Why'd you stop?"

Randy cringed at the breathy voice. How did Martha Lynn always manage to find him alone?

With an internal sigh, he watched her saunter into the barn. Her white blouse strained against her unsupported breasts. He could only imagine how the seams in her skirt ached.

She crouched next to him. He felt the heat rising from her body. The V in her shirt offered a generous view down her front.

He refocused his gaze back on his saxophone. "My heart's not in it," he replied to her question and her obvious invitation.

"Why not? Cassie Ann still giving you a hard time?"

When he was living in the city, it had never surprised him when some busybody added her two cents to the conversations he had with Cass. The walls were thin, and it was not too hard to hear a stray word or two, especially when someone pressed an ear against the material used to separate the apartments. But for news to travel so far and so fast in the country where the closest neighbor was over a mile away, the gossips had to be working overtime.

"If you ask me, the only person she has to be upset with is herself," Martha Lynn continued, though he hadn't asked.

Despite his resolve to keep what was between himself and Cass between Cass and him, his curiosity had him asking, "How so?"

"She was hanging out at the shipyard while you were home with *her* children."

Randy raised his head and cocked an eyebrow. How could Martha Lynn work side by side with her sister-in-law and then dismiss Cass's hard work?

"She should've been taking care of her house and her man like a good wife does." She stroked the bell of the saxophone. "Of course, that's the problem with most women. Once they got a man, they ignore his needs."

Her intentions could not be any clearer if she stretched a twelve-foot banner across the barn's entrance. Randy needed to remove himself from the situation…and fast.

He brushed her hand aside and closed the case. Gripping the handle, he stood. She rose with him and stood in his path.

"Why are you wasting your time in Piney Woods with Cassie Ann? You should be in New York, where people can appreciate your talents."

Knowing she would not understand, he did not bother to explain that Piney Woods was where Cass felt safe, and as long as she wanted to be there, he did not consider it a waste of time. He stepped to the side, and she moved with him.

"You don't belong here…and neither do I."

Certain she would block his way if he moved again, Randy decided it was time to make his position clear. A man who cheated on his wife was only one step above a bastard who believed it was within his right to take a firm hand to his spouse.

As he opened his mouth to inform her that she needed to look elsewhere for entertainment, Martha Lynn leaned in and pressed her soft lips to his. She tasted of peppermint, which from that moment forward, he would never be able to tolerate.

The roast he had consumed for supper turned in his stomach. He reached up, grabbed Martha Lynn by the shoulders and pushed her away from him.

She teetered on her heels for a heartbeat before landing on her butt with an "ooph."

Even before his mentor had stepped in and warned him to never lay a hand on a woman, Randy had considered it a sin. The many nights of listening to the sounds of fists striking flesh and the pleas for mercy, along with the daytime observations of his mother's black eyes and her beau's bruised knuckles, were enough to make him swear he would never lay a hand on a woman in anger. Yet he felt no remorse for his actions toward Martha Lynn.

"You ever try and come between Cass and me again…" He did not complete the threat for he did not know what he would do. The only thing he was certain of was he would not regret his actions.

Randy grabbed the case and stepped over Martha Lynn's outstretched legs. He marched out of the barn to the house. It was late enough that Cass would be getting the girls ready for bed. If he hurried, he would be able to hear their prayers.

He stepped onto the back porch and opened the door. The deep monotone voice used to soothe excited nerves filled the room as Cass's father read *The Three*

Little Pigs. The girls, dressed in their pajamas, sat on either side of their grandfather. They burst into a fit of giggles as the man huffed and puffed like the wolf.

While he enjoyed listening to the man entertain the children, Randy preferred Cass's wolf. No matter how hard she tried, she would never be able to elicit the same squeals from the girls as her father. At the same time, the deep, sultry tone never failed to put him in the mood for a little activity that would leave them huffing and puffing once they were done.

Randy turned to the bedroom and gaped at the emptiness. Cass never took off during the girls' bedtime. While they were living in Washington, D.C., it had been important to her that she saw her child off to bed and was there when she woke up in the morning. She had become more determined after leaving them with her parents while she worked in Norfolk.

"Out front," Mother Porter called out when her husband paused to turn the page of the book he was reading.

Randy placed his case against the wall and backed out of the room. He nodded his thanks to his mother-in-law before heading out the front door.

He stood in the middle of the porch and glanced into the dark. All was still, with the exception of two possums chasing each other across the empty field.

Randy turned to step back inside and ask if Cass had mentioned anything about a walk when, out of the corner of his eye, he noticed a flutter. He headed down the steps and continued around the house to the hickory tree.

Cass leaned against the trunk, facing the back of the house. Her spine became rigid as he got closer. She pushed away from the tree and raised her foot to move on.

"Before you run off to continue your vow of silence, please hear me out." Though she lowered her foot, she did not turn around. However, he would take what he could get. He moved behind her until he could smell the animal fat used to make the soap she used to wash the dishes. "I never meant for that night to happen."

"I know." Her voice was soft and even.

He flinched. "You do? Then why—"

"Am I still mad? 'Cause those men scared *my* babies."

"They're *my* babies, too," he clarified. "There's a part of me in those girls, and I'd do anythin' for them. Even leave."

He had not meant to blurt out the words. It was the last thing he wanted, but maybe it was time to stop fooling himself. He had tried to come home and pick up where they had left off, but there had been too many changes.

The words had been the toughest he ever uttered, but her reply could be the toughest he ever heard.

****

Cass spun around. Her lips moved, but no sound emerged.

She swore her ears were deceiving her. Randy had not suggested…he couldn't have…he wouldn't…

One, then two, then three seconds passed without a word, a grunt, or a peep from him. He simply stared down at her, shifting from one foot to another, not unlike an anxious boy waiting for a punishment.

Had her mother been right? Had her anger driven

her husband away? And what, if anything, could she do to make things right?

"I don't want you to leave," she whispered over the wind.

"Then what do you want?"

Out of all the questions he could have asked, that was the easiest one to answer, yet the hardest to achieve.

"I want everything to be the way it was before…"

Before the government took him away. Before the arguments. Before she no longer felt safe in her own home.

Chapter 16

"Motherf—" Randy jumped back to avoid the hammer that slipped from his grip. It smacked the plank an inch from his foot.

He would have patted himself on the back for the save if the hand he would have used had not been throbbing. Instead, he squeezed his eyes shut as his brain tried to work through the pain.

Avery's high-pitched, out-of-tune shrill had broken his concentration and the rhythm he had established seconds earlier. Startled, he'd glanced from his target and instantly regretted the action when the hammer smashed the knuckle on his index finger.

"What is your problem, chile?" Cass's canvas shoes squished in the mud as she walked from the back of the house to the porch where Randy had been repairing a chair. "Are you in pain?"

Certain she was not talking to him, he did not bother to unclench his teeth to answer.

"I was looking for Uncle Randy," Avery explained.

"You see him standing right there." The tools rattled when she tossed the hammer into the box he'd borrowed from his father-in-law. "What's wrong?"

"Mr. Simmons gave me a package for Uncle Randy."

He shuddered at the title by which Avery and June were forced to address their maternal grandfather. Yes, the man had been upset that his oldest grandchild was conceived out of wedlock, but that was not a reason to take it out on the child.

Randy opened his eyes and smiled at the girl struggling with the oversized package. Her sister shuffled up the road to the house, carrying schoolbooks for both of them.

"Mr. Simmons should be ashamed of himself. Making a girl carry a package instead of delivering it himself," Cass scolded as Randy stepped off the porch.

"It's not heavy." Avery passed the package to Randy. "What's in there?"

"Just 'cause you deliver the mail, it don't mean you need to know what's in it," Cass said. "Come inside, and I'll give you something for being helpful." She opened the screen door. "Also, I finished hemming your mother's dress. You can take that with you."

"Momma's not home," June announced.

"Then give it to her when she gets back."

"I don't know when that'll be," Avery added.

"What do you mean?"

The girl shrugged. "She left four days ago and hasn't returned."

Cass put her hand up, blocking the girl from entering the house. June, who was on her sister's heels, could not stop in time. She bounced off the older girl into Randy, who grabbed her collar before she stumbled down the steps.

"Your mother left four days ago with your father on the train to Nashville?" Cass asked.

"Yes, ma'am," Avery confirmed.

"Who's been watchin' after y'all?"

"I was." The twelve-year-old's voice was full of

pride. Randy did not fault her. She had taken care of her sister and herself and both survived the experience.

Cass's eyes darkened. She looked as if she would give anything to get five minutes with her sister-in-law.

"You cooked and watched after your sister?" she asked.

Avery shrugged as if the chores had been no big deal. "Been doing so since Daddy got home from the war."

"What did your mother do?" Randy asked.

"She hung out at the juke joint."

The woman had accused Cass of neglecting her family, while she ignored her daughters so she could go out and drink? Randy did not think he'd ever heard anything so hypocritical. At least his wife had been working to make sure her children had food in their stomachs and clothes on their backs.

Cass waved the girls into the house. "Y'all are staying here till Joe gets back."

"He got home last night," Avery said as she walked by her aunt.

Randy's shoulders grew heavier with the guilt that had been burdening him since they returned to Piney Woods. With the addition of the two girls, his wife's parents once again had a full house. And though the older couple did not complain, after raising six children of their own, they should be able to enjoy the freedom of walking around their small house without having to step over or bump into bodies.

He had hoped they would have found a solution to their problems by now, yet Cass had not answered the question Randy had posed to her two days earlier. And he was reluctant to push her for fear of what her answer would be.

****

"Figured you'd stop by." Joe Frank held out a beer as Randy climbed the steps to the small house the man rented from his parents. "What took you so long?"

Using the rail on the porch, Randy popped off the bottle cap. "Had some chores I wanted to finish." He dropped into the empty rocker next to his brother-in-law.

"Y'all need help over there?"

"It's just a few repairs. I can handle it."

The work helped pass the time until he—no, they—moved on. He refused to entertain thoughts of leaving Piney Woods without Cass and the girls.

"How are Cass and you getting along?" Joe Frank asked.

Randy took a healthy swig of his beer. He appreciated his brother-in-law's concern. But compared to the other man, his problems were minute.

"Things'll work out." He lowered his bottle and turned to Joe Frank. "How 'bout you? What happened?"

"Got in last night, and she wasn't here. When she didn't show this morning, I stopped by the juke joint she hung out at." He turned the bottle in his hand, picking loose the label. "They said she was there, telling everyone she was leaving for some place better."

Randy had figured all Martha Lynn's rambling about leaving was just talk and that after he rejected her advances she would return home and settle down.

"Are you sure she ran off?" he asked. "You looked around in case somethin' happened to her?"

"No doubt in my mind. Woman took off."

Joe Frank stared at the woods that separated his house from that of his parents. The man did not appear broken up by the fact that his wife was missing. Instead, he appeared content, as if it was just another Friday night.

If their situations were reversed, Randy would be tearing up the countryside searching for Cass. And if he could not find her, he would sure as hell need something stronger than a bottle of beer to numb the agonizing pain.

"After she got a taste of freedom, I knew she wouldn't be staying." Joe Frank chuckled. "Hell, I'm surprised she stayed this long."

"What do you mean?"

Joe Frank downed the remainder of his beer. "Martha Lynn was always chasing after a good time, and she found the perfect opportunity after I left. She didn't need to go to Norfolk to work. She wanted to run around, something Momma wasn't going to let her get away with up here."

"You're sayin' she didn't need to work?" Randy asked, thinking about Cass's insistence on taking a job while he was away. As frugal as she was, he had been certain they had enough saved up to sustain her until he returned.

"Of course not. She just wanted the freedom to party." Joe Frank leaned forward and set the bottle by his foot. "Now, don't you confuse my sister with that whore I married," the man said as if he could read Randy's thoughts. "Cass never gave you a reason not to trust her."

Randy could not refute that statement. When she'd worked at the club, Cass showed up for the show, and when it was over, she returned home without taking any detours. On the few occasions she did not go straight home, he was by her side. At the club, she had never flirted or given anyone a reason to misinterpret a word, glance, or gesture.

"Martha Lynn chased after nearly every man in Piney Woods." Joe Frank sat back with a fresh beer. He used the chair's arm to pop off the cap. "She even had her eye on you."

"Nothin' happened," Randy blurted, despite the kiss in the barn. He figured his declaration was not a lie since he'd pushed the woman away.

"I assumed you wouldn't do my sister like that." Joe Frank took a healthy swallow of his beer. "If I suspected otherwise, I'd have called you out on it by now."

A chill raced through Randy as his brother-in-law's tone turned serious. There was no doubt the man would have led the mob that included his other four brothers and his father.

"Only man that woman never chased after was me." Joe Frank's voice became wistful.

"If she didn't, then how did you…"

"Have two children?" Joe Frank completed the thought. "Only one belongs to me, and I'm not even a hundred percent sure about her."

"What are you sayin'?"

"Avery ain't mine."

"But you married 'cause she was carryin' Avery."

"I offered to marry her when she learned she was carrying. Everyone just assumed the rest."

"Why would you do that?"

Joe Frank snorted. "I always liked Martha Lynn.

Girl was pretty and feisty. But no matter how much I wooed her, she'd pay me no mind. I figured if I helped her out, she'd be grateful enough to care for me."

Randy recalled how distant Martha Lynn always was toward Joe Frank. She never acknowledged his presence or seemed like she gave a damn about him. Even the day he returned home from the war, she'd stood in the corner while everyone fussed over her husband.

"If she never warmed up to you, then what's the story with June?"

"One night I followed Martha Lynn to the juke joint. Don't remember much after polishing off that bottle of whiskey, but we woke up the next morning in bed together. Martha Lynn was so angry she was practically spitting fire. Said if anything came of that night, she'd get rid of it." Joe Frank gripped the bottle's neck. "My father taught me there was never an excuse to hit a woman, but that day I told Martha Lynn if she ever did anything to my baby, I'd turn her over my knee and tan her hide till God personally ordered me to stop."

Since that last meeting with Martha Lynn, Randy had been struggling with his inability to feel guilty for pushing a woman. After Joe Frank's confessions, he wondered how one woman could make men forget their morals.

"Guess for once she took me seriously. Nine months later she gave birth to June. Of course, she warned me after that day that I was never to lay a hand on her again."

Though he had no problem remaining faithful to Cass while he was in the service, Randy could not imagine going six years without being with a woman. "I'm sorry, man."

"Don't be. Figured she wasn't the only one who could have her needs taken care of away from home."

"That means—"

"I may be a saint for putting up with her, but I'm no monk. Been paying someone to take care of my needs for years." Joe Frank sighed. "Course it isn't the same as being with someone who cares about you."

Randy understood the sentiment. He had been with a number of women before he met Cass, but he'd never felt with them the same comfort or peace he experienced with his wife.

Maybe Martha Lynn's departure was a blessing for Joe Frank. He could move on from a loveless marriage and find someone who would make him happy.

"Does that mean…?"

Joe Frank simply nodded.

After a minute of silence, Randy suspected the man had met someone overseas but was not in the position to do something about their situation. Therefore, instead of forcing the man to dwell on a subject that appeared to bother him more than his wife's departure, he asked, "What do you plan to do now?"

"After I finish celebrating…?" Joe Frank shrugged his shoulders. "I figured after two years, things might be different, but I came back and everything was the same."

For Randy, it was the opposite. He had expected everything to be the same, yet too many things had changed.

****

Cass cringed at the sound of the toe smashing into

the trunk at the foot of the bed. Though she was safely curled up under the covers, her digit throbbed in empathy to her husband's pain.

Randy's foot smacked against the floor as he hopped to the side of the bed. With a growl, he plopped down onto the mattress.

"You're going to break your neck if you're not careful." She rolled over and rubbed the bare leg just below his boxers.

"Sorry I woke you."

"You didn't. I was already up."

"Dreams botherin' you?"

Despite the darkness, she shook her head as if he could see her. "Was worrying about Joe Frank."

Randy slid down next to her. "You should've gone with me."

Cass had been tempted to take him up on the offer when he originally made the suggestion after they tucked the girls into bed. She'd decided against joining the men, figuring they would want to talk amongst themselves.

"I'll see him in the morning."

"Till then, you're gonna worry."

"I'll be fine."

Randy pulled Cass to his side. "There's nothin' to worry about." He kissed the top of her head. "Joe'll be fine."

The inflection in his tone sounded like he was trying to convince himself. There was more that he was not telling her, and while she was curious, she would not ask him to betray her brother's trust.

Cass tossed the blanket to the side and pulled away from Randy.

"Where are you goin'?" he asked as she crawled around him.

"To check on the girls."

"I can assure you they're fine," he insisted when she stood.

"I just want—"

"Cass, please…" He grabbed the back of her nightgown. "Stop runnin' away from us."

She paused at his entreaty. She had two choices—continue to emotionally pull away from Randy until he followed Martha Lynn's example or turn to him for the comfort she sought.

Randy sat up and pulled her back until she stood between his legs. He then froze with his hands on her hips, and she knew the next move was hers.

Cass rested her hands on his shoulders. She leaned forward until her lips pressed against his. It had been two weeks since they had come together, which was two weeks too long. They needed each other; it was the only way they would be able to get through the trials life would throw at them.

Randy parted his lips. He tasted of tobacco and beer. Instead of being repulsed, she savored the sensation of his tongue caressing hers with the same rhythm his hands had as they kneaded her hips.

She thrust forward, needing to be closer to him. There was no need to pull back to tell him what she wanted. He took the cues from her reaction.

He slowly pushed up her gown until he could slip his hands underneath. She trembled at the feel of flesh on flesh. How could she deny herself his touch? When he reached for her, she should have come to him instead of pushing him away.

Cass needed Randy physically as well as emotionally, for it was his touch that reaffirmed just how much he cared for her. She pulled from the kiss, slipped the gown over her head, and dropped it to the floor. Her skin tingled as his warm hands released her.

He raised his hips just enough to slip his boxers to his thighs. Taking her wrist in his, he pulled her hand to him, letting her know he was more than ready to accommodate her.

Eager to be with him, she straddled his legs. Together they positioned him until she could ease down and take every inch of him within her.

She groaned; the last sound he permitted her to release. He covered her mouth with his, a wise move considering her parents were in the next bedroom and the girls were just outside the door that did not lock.

United, they moved together, just as they had promised they would do in life. They could enjoy the experience, but together it would be something magical.

Cass rocked against him as he thrust up. The smacking from flesh hitting flesh blended with the squeaking springs. The faint snores drifting from the other room indicated her father slept on despite the noise the made.

The pressure between her legs became more intense. It would soon be over, ending their risk of being heard.

Cass broke the kiss. Her head dropped forward; his neck muffled her whimpers. Her body shook with pleasure. She would never push him away again. She would turn to him in happiness and sadness. In sickness and in health. Till death did them part.

Randy tensed beneath her as he found his release.

He called the name of their maker. The blasphemy was music to her ears.

They remained still, long after their orgasms subsided. Clinging to each other, they offered and received the strength they would need to move forward.

Chapter 17

Randy had underplayed the situation. Joe Frank wasn't just fine; he was fabulous.

The man was glowing like someone who had just hit the numbers. There was an extra bounce in his step, and he was humming as he moved about the room, getting rid of everything that belonged to Martha Lynn.

In one quick motion, he swept his hand across the top of his wife's vanity and deposited the woman's makeup into a sack. He then spun around and crossed the room to the dresser. One by one he dropped the perfumes into the sack. The stench from the different fragrances blending together made Cass lightheaded.

"Woman was always wasting my money on crap," he mumbled as he tossed a jewelry box overflowing with colorful beads into the bag.

Cass fingered a gray silk dress draped over the back of the chair next to the door. A pink satin skirt was strewn across the seat with the matching blouse crumpled on the floor.

"What are you planning to do with these?" She picked up a gown that left little to the imagination.

"Take what you want."

When she was younger, Cass would have jumped at the opportunity to own the fine things Martha Lynn took for granted, but the dresses that hung precariously off wire hangers in the closet held no appeal to her.

They only reminded her of the person obsessed with material possessions; who would never value the loyalty of a good man or the admiration of her children.

"You paid for these..." He raised an eyebrow, and she clarified, "The money you earned paid for them. Don't you want to get the most use out of them?" She held up a blue silk blouse in her other hand. "These can be taken in for Avery."

Joe snatched the blouse out of her hand and shoved it into the bag. "My daughters will appreciate the feel of cotton against their skin and the hard work it takes to get that before they prance around in this shit."

Cass flinched. She'd had disagreements with Joe Frank in the past, but he had never raised his voice to her. Even after she ran off and married her first husband at sixteen, he'd only asked between clenched teeth if she had lost her everloving mind.

"I'm sorry, Joe."

"Dammit." He dropped the sack and took her hands in his. "Don't be. If anyone should be sorry, it should be me."

"Why?"

"I used to watch how trifling she was toward you when we were kids. Always walking around, showing off her store-bought clothes and tossing her fine hair. I knew she was trying to make you feel small 'cause all we could afford was the dresses Momma made from the material she got on sale. Yet I still married her."

"You were trying to do the right thing."

"Problem was I wasn't."

Cass wrinkled her brow. When was giving a child a name not the right thing? As she prepared to ask for an explanation, the bulb flickered on in her head. There were enough signs…from the shade of Avery's skin to the grade of her hair to her hazel eyes.

"When did you realize she wasn't yours?"

"Before I married her," he confessed. "I'd never been with anyone before then."

She pulled her hands from his and dropped onto the clothes on the chair. "Then why?"

"Even though she never showed any interest in me, I always wanted Martha Lynn. When I heard her parents kicked her out 'cause she was in a way, I offered to marry her in hopes she'd be grateful enough to give me the time of day."

While it was a poor excuse to marry someone, Cass could not criticize his decision. She had married her first husband because she thought he would show her the world. They only got as far as New York, where he had abandoned her two years later.

"We were married a year before I finally came to terms with the fact that she never did nor would ever give a damn about me." He plopped down on the edge of the bed. "At first I thought she was hesitant 'cause she was carrying, but six months after Avery was born, I decided to face the truth. It was me."

"Then why'd you stay?"

A silly smile spread across his face; the same one Randy wore whenever he spoke about his daughters. The expression said all she needed to know; he may not have made the girl, but Avery was his daughter, and he could not bring himself to leave her.

Cass's respect for her brother grew. She'd heard of men walking away from the children who were the spitting image of them. It took a special man to care that much for a child he knew wasn't his.

"What do you plan to do?" she asked, though she figured after staying in a loveless marriage for twelve years for the sake of a child that wasn't his, the chances of him giving up her or her sister were slim.

"I earned my GED while I was in the service." Joe Frank reached behind him and retrieved three brochures from under a pile of sheer nightgowns. "When I got back, I was thinking about applying for colleges up North."

"Why didn't you say anything?"

He shrugged as if it was no big deal, but in their family it was. Piney Woods only had one colored school in which all the grades, one through eight, sat in one room and were taught by the same teacher. None of their family or friends had a high school diploma or its equivalent.

"I didn't want to make a big deal about it in the event I didn't get in," Joe Frank said after a minute.

Cass understood. Though no one in their family would look down on him for not being accepted into a college, there were neighbors who would laugh at him for daring to dream.

"Now that Martha Lynn's taken off, I'm not sure." He shook his head. "I can't leave Avery and June with Momma while I take off to the city, and it'll be hard enough to support myself, much less two girls, while I'm studying."

Cass took the brochures from her brother. She hated the idea of him having to give up on a dream, especially one that could mean the difference not only for him but for his girls, too. If he moved from Piney Woods, Avery and June would have more options for their future.

She flipped through the first book and wondered. If he had talked to Martha Lynn about this, would the woman have stuck by his side and encouraged him? It was that moment she realized what had been missing from her relationship with Randy.

Before he had been drafted, they used to discuss their dreams and desires. Neither one of them would have told the other where they were going to live or work. Instead, they would have weighed the pros and cons of the situation and together would have made a decision that was best for the family.

Though it had been two years since they had done so, they needed to sit down as a couple and figure out what they wanted their future to hold.

****

Cass cringed at the god-awful noise. She ran the rest of the way to the barn to save whatever animal had its head caught in a pen.

She came to an abrupt stop at the door at the sight of Sylvia struggling through "Mary Had a Little Lamb" on a saxophone that was almost as big as she was. Randy stood beside the girl and flawlessly played along. The box that Avery had carried to the farm the previous day lay open next to Randy's case.

Cass stepped back from the doorway. It was the first time she had seen the girl relax around her father since his return. His face glowed as only a proud papa's would.

"How's that?" Sylvia asked when they finished the song.

Despite the off-key performance, Randy smiled at his daughter as if she had just performed a solo at Carnegie Hall. "Wonderful for your first try," he replied. "Now what are you supposed to do when you're finished?"

Sylvia placed her right leg behind her left and dropped down. Cass assumed the girl was supposed to curtsy; instead she ended up kneeling.

Randy applauded. "Bravo."

The man's praise pulled the corner of Cass's lips up.

"Are you ready for the most important lesson?"

"What's that?" Sylvia's eyes widened in anticipation.

"You must take care of your instrument."

"Why?"

"It will always reward you with beautiful notes if you take care of it."

Cass's heart expanded with pride. How could she ever doubt Randy's ability to care for the girl or her sister? He had patience and understanding that would eventually win any child over. And his love for the girls meant no one would get away with hurting them.

She stepped back as Randy went through the steps for disassembling the saxophone and cleaning it.

Cass missed performing with Randy—singing to him while he played for her. She longed to tell him through song what he meant to her, just as they used to do every afternoon when they rehearsed and again when they got on stage in the evening.

"Sylvia, come get cleaned up for lunch," Cass's mother called from the house, interrupting the father-daughter moment.

Cass stepped back into the doorway as Sylvia threw her arms around her father's neck and placed a sloppy kiss on his cheek. Randy held his daughter for a second before he pulled back and kissed her forehead.

"Go on," Randy said. "I'll finish up here."

Sylvia released her father and dashed out of the barn without acknowledging Cass. "Grandma, I was playin' the saxophone," she screamed. "And Daddy said I was wonderful."

Cass chuckled at the girl's enthusiasm. "Where'd you get that?" she asked.

"I wrote Eli askin' if he knew someone sellin' a sax, and he sent me Mannie's," he replied, referring to Eli Viera, a friend in New York. Eli and his wife had served as witnesses when Randy and Cass got married.

"I take it Mannie lost interest in playing the instrument."

"Said the boy didn't have it a week before he decided he wanted to play the drums."

"So how much does he want for it?"

"Nothin'. He told us to consider it a belated birthday present for Sylvia."

Cass knelt next to Randy and examined the saxophone. It was a generous gift. The instrument was so new it barely had any fingerprints on it.

"How's the family?"

"He and Flo are expectin' another child in June; he's thinkin' about openin' a club, and Mannie doesn't like school…"

"Wait a minute. Back up."

"To the news about Flo expectin'?"

"No, the news you squeezed in between the happy announcement and the information I don't give a damn about."

Randy closed both cases. "Eli wants to open a club."

Suspecting Eli would not have written to discuss his plans unless there was more to it, she added, "And?"

He stood and Cass followed his example. She waited until he placed both cases by the door, returned to her side, and surrounded her hand with his.

"Come." Randy led her out the barn toward the field where she used to work after school in the spring and fall and all day during summer as a child.

While she worked, Cass would daydream about the places she read about—wishing she would one day have the opportunity to travel to different locations and meet new people. But like Joe Frank, she kept her dreams to herself. What would she achieve by revealing a wish she did not have the resources to grant?

"The last time Eli visited D.C., he asked me to consider goin' into business with him," Randy said, reminding Cass why they were taking the walk. "At the time I wasn't sure. You'd just announced you were pregnant again, and we had the steady gig at the Panama Lounge. But now…"

Randy's admission had come as a surprise. Cass had expected him to say Eli wanted them to perform at the club, not own part of it.

"What do you know about running a club?"

"Not much…"

Randy's confession did not inspire confidence in Cass. Yet she suspected their friend would not have broached the subject if he did not believe Randy could contribute something to the business's success.

While a club was a big—and, if it failed, costly—investment, Cass could not think of a reason why they should not consider it. They had a sizable savings, thanks to smart financial planning before Randy had been drafted and her insistence on working instead of touching the money while he was away. Neither of them had a commitment to another club.

As for their living arrangements, as much as Cass enjoyed being around her family, the move south was supposed to have been temporary, only until Randy had returned from the service. She wanted to be someplace where she could not only perform with her husband but acknowledge their relationship as well.

Cass saw the proposal as the topic they needed to open the lines of communication that had shut down between them.

Chapter 18

Randy had never been able to stand a woman's tears, but in Mother Porter's case, he was willing to make an exception, since, he hoped, her tears were ones of joy regarding his new business venture. He hated to think she was upset over him taking her daughter and grandchildren away from her.

Sylvia turned from her grandmother to Randy. Her internal conflict was evident in the round, hazel orbs that stared up at him. She wanted to comfort the woman, yet she was reluctant to leave his side in the event he should wander to the barn and start practicing the saxophone without her.

Randy gave her shoulder a reassuring squeeze. He rubbed Shara's back with his other hand. The gesture calmed the girl, who shoved her thumb into her mouth and laid her head on his chest.

Cass sat on the sofa next to her mother and pushed a handkerchief into the woman's hand. "Please tell me those are tears of joy," she admonished, addressing the question on everyone's mind.

"Yes, I'm happy for you." Mother Porter dabbed her eyes with the cloth and added, "But I'll be lying if I said I wouldn't miss you." She patted Cass's knee. "When are you plannin' to leave?"

"At the end of the week," Randy replied.

"So soon? Everything's happenin' so fast."

He silently disagreed. It had been three months since he proposed to Cass the idea of opening a club. After weighing the pros and cons of starting a business, they drove north to continue the discussion with their business partners.

Once all questions had been answered and worries eased, Cass returned to Piney Woods. Randy stayed with their friends in New York while he took care of the paperwork needed to secure a loan through the G.I. bill for the business and start renovation on the space they had chosen.

He kept Cass updated on the progress through his weekly letters. And once enough work had been completed that he had the time to focus on the next step, she returned to the city to help search for a place they could call home.

"Well, at least all my boys are down here," Mother Porter said.

Cass glanced up at Joe Frank, who stood next to her, avoiding eye contact with all the women. After a heartbeat, she pinched her sibling's leg.

"Dammit, woman," Joe Frank said, jumping out of his sister's reach.

"Watch your language," Mother Porter scolded.

"Sorry, Momma."

"What has gotten into you?"

Joe Frank glared at Cass, while rubbing the tender spot on his leg. When he failed to reply, Cass offered, "He has something to tell you, Momma," which reminded Randy of a brat tattling on her brother.

"What is it?"

With every eye in the room on him, Joe Frank could not back down. After mouthing a threat of payback, he took a deep breath and announced, "I'm going with them."

"You are? But why?"

"I'm going to college, Momma."

The silence that filled the room seemed to extend across the entire farm. For two seconds, no one uttered a sound as Cass stared up at her brother with pride, while he shifted from one foot to another, waiting for his mother's reply.

"College?" the woman whispered. "My baby boy's goin' to college."

Randy had a hard time stifling his laughter. Her baby boy was in his thirties; he towered over her, and he was a father of two. But of course Cass had no problem speaking her mind.

"That's the biggest baby I've ever seen."

Joe Frank retaliated by pulling the braid hanging between his sister's shoulder blades.

"Ouch, dammit."

"Cassie Ann Jones, watch your mouth."

The woman mumbled her apology as she glared at her brother. Before she could promise revenge, her father stepped between the siblings and congratulated his son.

"If you're goin' to school, where do you plan on livin'?" Mother Porter asked.

"The house we bought is big enough for all of us."

When Cass first proposed the idea of all of them living under one roof, Randy could tell she had a speech prepared. She, however, did not have to go farther than, "I'd like Joe Frank to live with us," before he agreed.

After everything they had done for him, from

welcoming him into the clan to offering him a place to stay when he had nowhere else to go, Cass's family would always be welcome in his home.

Avery plopped down in the empty space next to her grandmother and informed her of everything she had been told about the new house. Not to be left out, June climbed onto her sister's lap and confirmed the information with a nod for every detail.

Sylvia raced across the room and squeezed between her mother and grandmother. Her sister slid off Randy's lap and followed, stopping in front of her mother, staring at her until she relinquished her spot on the sofa to the girl.

Cass went to Randy's side. He slipped his arm around her waist and held her close.

"Excited?" he asked.

"More like nervous," she replied.

"You know, it's not too late to back out."

****

Cass shook her head.

She had considered the money they would lose if the business failed. However, what would be the purpose of leaving if she was not willing to take a chance? If she was only going to play it safe, she might as well stay where she was.

Unlike the last time she left home, she was not tagging behind someone who was full of talk about the adventures but had never been farther than his own back yard. Nor was she with someone content to make excuses instead of working overtime to get ahead.

This time, she was going to be with someone who had proven he was willing to honor his vows to love and cherish her through good times and bad.

Ursula Renée

A word about the author...

Ursula Renée writes historical fiction and romances set between the roaring twenties and the disco era.

She is a member of Romance Writers of America, Sisters in Crime, Mystery Writers of America, and The Historical Novel Society.

When she is not writing, Ursula enjoys photography, drawing, and stone carving. She is the mother to one son and two cats.

Thank you for purchasing
this publication of The Wild Rose Press, Inc.

If you enjoyed the story, we would appreciate your
letting others know by leaving a review.

For other wonderful stories,
please visit our on-line bookstore at
www.thewildrosepress.com.

For questions or more information
contact us at
info@thewildrosepress.com.

The Wild Rose Press, Inc.
www.thewildrosepress.com

Stay current with The Wild Rose Press, Inc.

Like us on Facebook

https://www.facebook.com/TheWildRosePress

And Follow us on Twitter
https://twitter.com/WildRosePress